Black Rock

Ralph Connor

Contents

BLACK ROCK

BY

Ralph Connor

BLACK ROCK
A TALE OF THE SELKIRKS
By Ralph Connor

INTRODUCTION

I think I have met "Ralph Conner." Indeed, I am sure I have--once in a canoe on the Red River, once on the Assinaboine, and twice or thrice on the prairies to the West. That was not the name he gave me, but, if I am right, it covers one of the most honest and genial of the strong characters that are fighting the devil and doing good work for men all over the world. He has seen with his own eyes the life which he describes in this book, and has himself, for some years of hard and lonely toil, assisted in the good influences which he traces among its wild and often hopeless conditions. He writes with the freshness and accuracy of an eye-witness, with the style (as I think his readers will allow) of a real artist, and with the tenderness and hopefulness of a man not only of faith but of experience, who has seen in fulfillment the ideals for which he lives.

The life to which he takes us, though far off and very strange to our tame minds, is the life of our brothers. Into the Northwest of Canada the young men of Great Britain and Ireland have been pouring (I was told), sometimes at the rate of 48,000 a year. Our brothers who left home yesterday--our hearts cannot but follow them. With these pages Ralph Conner enables our eyes and our minds to follow, too; nor do I think there is any one who shall read this book and not find also that his conscience is quickened. There is a warfare appointed unto man upon earth, and its struggles are nowhere more intense, nor the victories of the strong, nor the succors brought to the fallen, more heroic, than on the fields described in this volume.

GEORGE ADAM SMITH.

BLACK ROCK

The story of the book is true, and chief of the failures in the making of the book is this, that it is not all the truth. The light is not bright enough, the shadow is not black enough to give a true picture of that bit of Western life of which the writer was some small part. The men of the book are still there in the mines and lumber camps of the mountains, fighting out that eternal fight for manhood, strong, clean, God-conquered. And, when the west winds blow, to the open ear the sounds of battle come, telling the fortunes of the fight.

Because a man's life is all he has, and because the only hope of the brave young West lies in its men, this story is told. It may be that the tragic pity of a broken life may move some to pray, and that that divine power there is in a single brave heart to summon forth hope and courage may move some to fight. If so, the tale is not told in vain.

C.W.G.

CHAPTER I
CHRISTMAS EVE IN A LUMBER CAMP

It was due to a mysterious dispensation of Providence, and a good deal to Leslie Graeme, that I found myself in the heart of the Selkirks for my Christmas Eve as the year 1882 was dying. It had been my plan to spend my Christmas far away in Toronto, with such Bohemian and boon companions as could be found in that cosmopolitan and kindly city. But Leslie Graeme changed all that, for, discovering me in the village of Black Rock, with my traps all packed, waiting for the stage to start for the Landing, thirty miles away, he bore down upon me with resistless force, and I found myself recovering from my surprise only after we had gone in his lumber sleigh some six miles on our way to his camp up in the mountains. I was surprised and much delighted, though I would not allow him to think so, to find that his old-time power over me was still there. He could always in the old 'Varsity days--dear, wild days--make me do what he liked. He was so handsome and so reckless, brilliant in his class-work, and the prince of half-backs on the Rugby field, and with such power of fascination, as would 'extract the heart out of a wheelbarrow,' as Barney Lundy used to say. And thus it was that I found myself just three weeks later--I was to have spent two or three days,--on the afternoon of the 24th of December, standing in Graeme's Lumber Camp No. 2, wondering at myself. But I did not regret my changed plans, for in those three weeks I had raided a cinnamon bear's den and had wakened up a grizzly--But I shall let the grizzly finish the tale; he probably sees more humour in it than I.

The camp stood in a little clearing, and consisted of a group of three long, low shanties with smaller shacks near them, all built of heavy, unhewn logs, with door and window in each. The grub camp, with cook-shed attached, stood in the middle of the clearing; at a little distance was the sleeping-camp with the office built against it, and about a hundred yards away on the other side of the clearing stood the stables, and near them the smiddy. The mountains rose grandly on every side, throwing up their great peaks into the sky. The clearing in which the camp stood was hewn out of a dense pine forest that filled the valley and climbed half way up the mountain-sides, and then frayed out in scattered and stunted trees.

It was one of those wonderful Canadian winter days, bright, and with a touch of sharpness in the air that did not chill, but warmed the blood like draughts of wine. The men were up in the woods, and the shrill scream of the blue jay flashing across the open, the impudent chatter of the red squirrel from the top of the grub camp, and the pert chirp of the whisky-jack, hopping about on the rubbish-heap, with the long, lone cry of the wolf far down the valley, only made the silence felt the more.

As I stood drinking in with all my soul the glorious beauty and the silence of mountain and forest, with the Christmas feeling stealing into me, Graeme came out from his office, and, catching sight of me, called out, 'Glorious Christmas weather, old chap!' And then, coming nearer, 'Must you go to-morrow?'

'I fear so,' I replied, knowing well that the Christmas feeling was on him too.

'I wish I were going with you,' he said quietly.

I turned eagerly to persuade him, but at the look of suffering in his face the words died at my lips, for we both were thinking of the awful night of horror when all his bright, brilliant life crashed down about him in black ruin and shame. I could only throw my arm over his shoulder and stand silent beside him. A sudden jingle of bells roused him, and, giving himself a little shake, he exclaimed, 'There are the boys coming home.'

Soon the camp was filled with men talking, laughing, chaffing, like light-hearted boys.

'They are a little wild to-night,' said Graeme; 'and to morrow they'll paint Black Rock red.'

Before many minutes had gone, the last teamster was 'washed up,' and all were standing about waiting impatiently for the cook's signal--the supper to-night was to be 'something of a feed'--when the sound of bells drew their attention to a light sleigh drawn by a buckskin broncho coming down the hillside at a great pace.

'The preacher, I'll bet, by his driving,' said one of the men.

'Bedad, and it's him has the foine nose for turkey!' said Blaney, a good-natured, jovial Irishman.

'Yes, or for pay-day, more like,' said Keefe, a black-browed, villainous fellow-countryman of Blaney's, and, strange to say, his great friend.

Big Sandy M'Naughton, a Canadian Highlander from Glengarry, rose up in wrath. 'Bill Keefe,' said he, with deliberate emphasis, 'you'll just keep your dirty tongue off the minister; and as for your pay, it's little he sees of it, or any one else, except Mike Slavin, when you're too dry to wait for some one to treat you, or perhaps Father Ryan, when the fear of hell-fire is on to you.'

The men stood amazed at Sandy's sudden anger and length of speech.

'Bon; dat's good for you, my bully boy,' said Baptiste, a wiry little French-Canadian, Sandy's sworn ally and devoted admirer ever since the day when the big Scotsman, under great provocation, had knocked him clean off the dump into the river and then jumped in for him.

It was not till afterwards I learned the cause of Sandy's sudden wrath which urged him to such unwonted length of speech. It was not simply that the Presbyterian blood carried with it reverence for the minister and contempt for Papists and Fenians, but that he had a vivid remembrance of how, only a month ago, the minister had got him out of Mike Slavin's saloon and out the clutches of Keefe and Slavin and their gang of bloodsuckers.

Keefe started up with a curse. Baptiste sprang to Sandy's side, slapped him on the back, and called out, 'You keel him, I'll hit (eat) him up, me.'

It looked as if there might be a fight, when a harsh voice said in a low, savage tone, 'Stop your row, you blank fools; settle it, if you want to, somewhere else.' I turned, and was amazed to see old man Nelson, who was very seldom moved to speech.

There was a look of scorn on his hard, iron-grey face, and of such settled fierceness as made me quite believe the tales I had heard of his deadly fights in the mines at the coast. Before any reply could be made, the minister drove up and called out in a cheery voice, 'Merry Christmas, boys! Hello, Sandy! Comment ca va, Baptiste? How do you do, Mr. Graeme?'

'First rate. Let me introduce my friend, Mr. Connor, sometime medical student, now artist, hunter, and tramp at large, but not a bad sort.'

'A man to be envied,' said the minister, smiling. 'I am glad to know any friend of Mr. Graeme's.'

I liked Mr. Craig from the first. He had good eyes that looked straight out at you, a clean-cut, strong face well set on his shoulders, and altogether an upstanding, manly bearing. He insisted on going with Sandy to the stables to see Dandy, his broncho, put up.

'Decent fellow,' said Graeme; 'but though he is good enough to his broncho, it is Sandy that's in his mind now.'

'Does he come out often? I mean, are you part of his parish, so to speak?'

'I have no doubt he thinks so; and I'm blowed if he doesn't make the Presbyterians of us think so too.' And he added after a pause, 'A dandy lot of parishioners we are for any man. There's Sandy, now, he would knock Keefe's head off as a kind of religious exercise; but to-morrow Keefe will be sober, and Sandy will be drunk as a lord, and the drunker he is the better Presbyterian he'll be; to the preacher's disgust.' Then after another pause he added bitterly, 'But it is not for me to throw rocks at Sandy; I am not the same kind of fool, but I am a fool of several other sorts.'

Then the cook came out and beat a tattoo on the bottom of a dish-pan. Baptiste answered with a yell: but though keenly hungry, no man would demean himself to do other than walk with apparent reluctance to his place at the table. At the further end of the camp was a big fireplace, and from the door to the fireplace extended the long board tables, covered with platters of turkey not too scientifically carved, dishes of potatoes, bowls of apple sauce, plates of butter, pies, and smaller dishes distributed at regular intervals. Two lanterns hanging from the roof, and a row of candles stuck into the wall on either side by means of slit sticks, cast a dim, weird light over the scene.

There was a moment's silence, and at a nod from Graeme Mr. Craig rose and said, 'I don't know how you feel about it, men, but to me this looks good enough to be thankful for.'

'Fire ahead, sir,' called out a voice quite respectfully, and the minister bent his head and said-- 'For Christ the Lord who came to save us, for all the love and goodness we have known, and for these Thy gifts to us this Christmas night, our Father, make us thankful. Amen.'

'Bon, dat's fuss rate,' said Baptiste. 'Seems lak dat's make me hit (eat) more better for sure,' and then no word was spoken for quarter of an hour. The occasion was far too solemn and moments too precious for anything so empty as words. But when the white piles of bread and the brown piles of turkey had for a second time vanished, and after the last pie had disappeared, there came a pause and hush of expectancy, whereupon the cook and cookee, each bearing aloft a huge, blazing pudding, came forth.

'Hooray!' yelled Blaney, 'up wid yez!' and grabbing the cook by the shoulders from behind, he faced him about.

Mr. Craig was the first to respond, and seizing the cookee in the same way, called out, 'Squad, fall in! quick march!' In a moment every man was in the procession.

'Strike up, Batchees, ye little angel!' shouted Blaney, the appellation a concession to the minister's presence; and away went Baptiste in a rollicking French song with the English chorus--

> 'Then blow, ye winds, in the morning,
> Blow, ye winds, ay oh!
> Blow, ye winds, in the morning,
> Blow, blow, blow.'

And at each 'blow' every boot came down with a thump on the plank floor that shook the solid roof. After the second round, Mr. Craig jumped upon the bench, and called out--

'Three cheers for Billy the cook!'

In the silence following the cheers Baptiste was heard to say, 'Bon! dat's mak me feel lak hit dat puddin' all hup mesef, me.'

'Hear till the little baste!' said Blaney in disgust.

'Batchees,' remonstrated Sandy gravely, 'ye've more stomach than manners.'

'Fu sure! but de more stomach dat's more better for dis puddin',' replied the little Frenchman cheerfully.

After a time the tables were cleared and pushed back to the wall, and pipes were produced. In all attitudes suggestive of comfort the men disposed themselves in a wide circle about the fire, which now roared and crackled up the great wooden chimney hanging from the roof. The lumberman's hour of bliss had arrived. Even old man Nelson looked a shade less melancholy than usual as he sat alone, well away from the fire, smoking steadily and silently. When the second pipes were well a-going, one of the men took down a violin from the wall and handed it to Lachlan Campbell. There were two brothers Campbell just out from Argyll, typical Highlanders: Lachlan, dark, silent, melancholy, with the face of a mystic, and Angus, red-haired, quick, impulsive, and devoted to his brother, a devotion he thought proper to cover under biting, sarcastic speech.

Lachlan, after much protestation, interspersed with gibes from his brother, took the violin, and, in response to the call from all sides, struck up 'Lord Macdonald's Reel.' In a moment the floor was filled with dancers, whooping and cracking their fingers in the wildest manner. Then Baptiste did the 'Red River Jig,' a most intricate and difficult series of steps, the men keeping time to the music with hands and feet.

When the jig was finished, Sandy called for 'Lochaber No More'; but Campbell said, 'No, no! I cannot play that to-night. Mr. Craig will play.'

Craig took the violin, and at the first note I knew he was no ordinary player. I did not recognise the music, but it was soft and thrilling, and got in by the heart, till every one was thinking his tenderest and saddest thoughts.

After he had played two or three exquisite bits, he gave Campbell his violin, saying, 'Now, "Lochaber," Lachlan.'

Without a word Lachlan began, not 'Lochaber'--he was not ready for that yet--but 'The Flowers o' the Forest,' and from that wandered through 'Auld Robin Gray' and 'The Land o' the Leal,' and so got at last to that most soul-subduing of Scottish laments, 'Lochaber No More.' At the first strain, his brother, who had thrown himself on some blankets behind the fire, turned over on his face, feigning sleep. Sandy M'Naughton took his pipe out of his mouth, and sat up straight and stiff, staring into vacancy, and Graeme, beyond the fire, drew a short, sharp breath. We had often sat, Graeme and I, in our student-days, in the drawing-room at home, listening to his father wailing out 'Lochaber' upon the pipes, and I well knew that the awful minor strains were now eating their way into his soul.

Over and over again the Highlander played his lament. He had long since forgotten us, and was seeing visions of the hills and lochs and glens of his far-away native land, and making us, too, see strange things out of the dim past. I glanced at old man Nelson, and was startled at the eager, almost piteous, look in his eyes, and I wished Campbell would stop. Mr. Craig caught my eye, and, stepping over to Campbell, held out his hand for the violin. Lingeringly and lovingly the Highlander drew out the last strain, and silently gave the minister his instrument.

Without a moment's pause, and while the spell of 'Lochaber' was still upon us, the minister, with exquisite skill, fell into the refrain of that simple and beautiful camp-meeting hymn, 'The Sweet By and By.' After playing the verse through once, he sang softly the refrain. After the first verse, the men joined in the chorus; at first timidly, but by the time the third verse was reached they were shouting with throats full open, 'We shall meet on that beautiful shore.' When I looked at Nelson the eager light had gone out of his eyes, and in its place was kind of determined hopelessness, as if in this new music he had no part.

After the voices had ceased, Mr. Craig played again the refrain, more and more softly and slowly; then laying the violin on Campbell's knees, he drew from his pocket his little Bible, and said--

'Men, with Mr. Graeme's permission, I want to read you something this Christmas Eve. You will all have heard it before, but you will like it none the less for that.'

His voice was soft, but clear and penetrating, as he read the eternal story of the angels and the shepherds and the Babe. And as he read, a slight motion of the hand or a glance of an eye made us see, as he was seeing, that whole radiant drama. The wonder, the timid joy, the tenderness, the mystery of it all, were borne in upon us with overpowering effect. He closed the book, and in the same low, clear voice went on to tell us how, in his home years ago, he used to stand on Christmas Eve listening in thrilling delight to his mother telling him the story, and how she used to make him see the shepherds and hear the sheep bleating near by, and how the sudden burst of glory used to make his heart jump.

'I used to be a little afraid of the angels, because a boy told me they were ghosts; but my mother told me better, and I didn't fear them any more. And the Baby, the dear little Baby--we all love a baby.' There was a quick, dry sob; it was from Nelson. 'I used to peek through under to see the little one in the straw, and wonder what things swaddling clothes were. Oh, it was all so real and so beautiful!' He paused, and I could hear the men breathing.

'But one Christmas Eve,' he went on, in a lower, sweeter tone, 'there was no one to tell me the story, and I grew to forget it, and went away to college, and learned to think that it was only a child's tale and was not for men. Then bad days came to me and worse, and I began to lose my grip of myself, of life, of hope, of goodness, till one black Christmas, in the slums of a faraway city, when I had given up all, and the devil's arms were about me, I heard the story again. And as I listened, with a bitter ache in my heart, for I had put it all behind me, I suddenly found myself peeking under the shepherds' arms with a child's wonder at the Baby in the straw. Then it came over me like great waves, that His name was Jesus, because it was He that should save men from their sins. Save! Save! The waves kept beating upon my ears, and before I knew, I had called out, "Oh! can He save me?" It was in a little mission meeting on one of the side streets, and they seemed to be used to that sort of thing there, for no one was surprised; and a young fellow leaned across the aisle to me and said, "Why! you just bet He can!" His surprise that I should doubt, his bright face and confident tone, gave me hope that perhaps it might be so. I held to that hope with all my soul, and'--stretching up his arms, and with a quick glow in his face and a little break in his voice, 'He hasn't failed me yet; not once, not once!'

He stopped quite short, and I felt a good deal like making a fool of myself, for in those days I had not made up my mind about these things. Graeme, poor old chap, was gazing at him with a sad yearning in his dark eyes; big Sandy was sitting very stiff, and staring harder than ever into the fire; Baptiste was trembling with excitement; Blaney was openly wiping the tears away. But the face that held my eyes was that of old man Nelson. It was white, fierce, hungry-looking, his sunken eyes burning, his lips parted as if to cry.

The minister went on. 'I didn't mean to tell you this, men, it all came over me with a rush; but it is true, every word, and not a word will I take back. And, what's more, I can tell you this, what He did for me He can do for any man, and it doesn't make any difference what's behind him, and'--leaning slightly forward, and with a little thrill of pathos vibrating in his voice--'O boys, why don't you give Him a chance at you? Without Him you'll never be the men you want to be, and you'll never get the better of that that's keeping some of you now from going back home. You know you'll never go back till you're the men you want to be.' Then, lifting up his face and throwing back his head, he said, as if to himself, 'Jesus! He shall save His people from their sins,' and then, 'Let us pray.'

Graeme leaned forward with his face in his hands; Baptiste and Blaney dropped on their knees; Sandy, the Campbells, and some others, stood up. Old man Nelson held his eyes steadily on the minister.

Only once before had I seen that look on a human face. A young fellow had broken through the ice on the river at home, and as the black water was dragging his fingers one by one from the slippery edges, there came over his face that same look. I used to wake up for many a night after in a sweat of horror, seeing the white face with its parting lips, and its piteous, dumb appeal, and the black water slowly sucking it down.

Nelson's face brought it all back; but during the prayer the face changed, and seemed to settle into resolve of some sort, stern, almost gloomy, as of a man with his last chance before him.

After the prayer Mr. Craig invited the men to a Christmas dinner next day in Black Rock. 'And because you are an independent lot, we'll charge you half a dollar for dinner and the evening show.' Then leaving a bundle of magazines and illustrated papers on the table--a godsend to the men--he said good-bye and went out.

I was to go with the minister, so I jumped into the sleigh first, and waited while he said good-bye to Graeme, who had been hard hit by the whole service, and seemed to want to say something. I heard Mr. Craig say cheerfully and confidently, 'It's a true bill: try Him.'

Sandy, who had been steadying Dandy while that interesting broncho was attempting with great success to balance himself on his hind legs, came to say good-bye. 'Come and see me first thing, Sandy.'

'Ay! I know; I'll see ye, Mr. Craig,' said Sandy earnestly, as Dandy dashed off at a full gallop across the clearing and over the bridge, steadying down when he reached the hill.

'Steady, you idiot!'

This was to Dandy, who had taken a sudden side spring into the deep snow, almost upsetting us. A man stepped out from the shadow. It was old man Nelson. He came straight to the sleigh, and, ignoring my presence completely, said--

'Mr. Craig, are you dead sure of this? Will it work?'

'Do you mean,' said Craig, taking him up promptly, 'can Jesus Christ save you from your sins and make a man of you?'

The old man nodded, keeping his hungry eyes on the other's face.

'Well, here's His message to you: "The Son of Man is come to seek and to save that which was lost."'

'To me? To me?' said the old man eagerly.

'Listen; this, too, is His Word: "Him that cometh unto Me I will in no wise cast out." That's for you, for here you are, coming.'

'You don't know me, Mr. Craig. I left my baby fifteen years ago because--'

'Stop!' said the minister. 'Don't tell me, at least not to-night; perhaps never. Tell Him who knows it all now, and who never betrays a secret. Have it out with Him. Don't be afraid to trust Him.'

Nelson looked at him, with his face quivering, and said in a husky voice, 'If this is no good, it's hell for me.'

'If it is no good,' replied Craig, almost sternly, 'it's hell for all of us.'

The old man straightened himself up, looked up at the stars, then back at Mr. Craig, then at me, and, drawing a deep breath, said, 'I'll try Him.' As he was turning away the minister touched him on the arm, and said quietly, 'Keep an eye on Sandy to-morrow.'

Nelson nodded, and we went on; but before we took the next turn I looked back and saw what brought a lump into my throat. It was old man Nelson on his knees in the snow, with his hands spread upward to the stars, and I wondered if there was any One above the stars, and nearer than the stars, who could see. And then the trees hid him from my sight

CHAPTER II
THE BLACK ROCK CHRISTMAS

Many strange Christmas Days have I seen, but that wild Black Rock Christmas stands out strangest of all. While I was revelling in my delicious second morning sleep, just awake enough to enjoy it, Mr. Craig came abruptly, announcing breakfast and adding, 'Hope you are in good shape, for we have our work before us this day.'

'Hello!' I replied, still half asleep, and anxious to hide from the minister that I was trying to gain a few more moments of snoozing delight, 'what's abroad?'.

'The devil,' he answered shortly, and with such emphasis that I sat bolt upright, looking anxiously about.

'Oh! no need for alarm. He's not after you particularly--at least not to-day,' said Craig, with a shadow of a smile. 'But he is going about in good style, I can tell you.'

By this time I was quite awake. 'Well, what particular style does His Majesty affect this morning?'

He pulled out a showbill. 'Peculiarly gaudy and effective, is it not?'

The items announced were sufficiently attractive. The 'Frisco Opera Company were to produce the 'screaming farce,' 'The Gay and Giddy Dude'; after which there was to be a 'Grand Ball,' during which the 'Kalifornia Female Kickers' were to do some fancy figures; the whole to be followed by a 'big supper' with 'two free drinks to every man and one to the lady,' and all for the insignificant sum of two dollars.

'Can't you go one better?' I said.

He looked inquiringly and a little disgustedly at me.

'What can you do against free drinks and a dance, not to speak of the "High Kickers"?' he groaned.

'No!' he continued; 'it's a clean beat for us today. The miners and lumbermen will have in their pockets ten thousand dollars, and every dollar burning a hole; and Slavin and his gang will get most of it. But,' he added, 'you must have breakfast. You'll find a tub in the kitchen; don't be afraid to splash. It is the best I have to offer you.'

The tub sounded inviting, and before many minutes had passed I was in a delightful glow, the effect of cold water and a rough towel, and that consciousness of virtue that comes to a man who has had courage to face his cold bath on a winter morning.

The breakfast was laid with fine taste. A diminutive pine-tree, in a pot hung round with wintergreen, stood in the centre of the table.

'Well, now, this looks good; porridge, beefsteak, potatoes, toast, and marmalade.'

'I hope you will enjoy it all.'

There was not much talk over our meal. Mr. Craig was evidently preoccupied, and as blue as his politeness would allow him. Slavin's victory weighed upon his spirits. Finally he burst out, 'Look here! I can't, I won't stand it; something must be done. Last Christmas this town was for two weeks, as one of the miners said, "a little suburb of hell." It was something too awful. And at the end of it all one young fellow was found dead in his shack, and twenty or more crawled back to the camps, leaving their three months' pay with Slavin and his suckers.

'I won't stand it, I say.' He turned fiercely on me. 'What's to be done?'

This rather took me aback, for I had troubled myself with nothing of this sort in my life before, being fully occupied in keeping myself out of difficulty, and allowing others the same privilege. So I ventured the consolation that he had done his part, and that a spree more or less would not make much difference to these men. But the next moment I wished I had been slower in speech, for he swiftly faced me, and his words came like a torrent.

'God forgive you that heartless word! Do you know--? But no; you don't know what you are saying. You don't know that these men have been clambering for dear life out of a fearful pit for three months past, and doing good climbing too, poor chaps. You don't think that some of them have wives, most of them mothers and sisters, in the east or across the sea, for whose sake they are slaving here; the miners hoping to save enough to bring their families to this homeless place, the rest to make enough to go back with credit. Why, there's Nixon, miner, splendid chap; has been here for two years, and drawing the highest pay. Twice he has been in sight of his heaven, for he can't speak of his wife and babies without breaking up, and twice that slick son of the devil--that's Scripture, mind you--Slavin, got him, and "rolled" him, as the boys say. He went back to the mines broken in body and in heart. He says this is his third and last chance. If Slavin gets him, his wife and babies will never see him on earth or in heaven. There is Sandy, too, and the rest. And,' he added, in a lower tone, and with the curious little thrill of pathos in his voice, 'this is the day the Saviour came to the world.' He paused, and then with a little sad smile, 'But I don't want to abuse you.'

'Do, I enjoy it, I'm a beast, a selfish beast'; for somehow his intense, blazing earnestness made me feel uncomfortably small.

'What have we to offer?' I demanded.

'Wait till I have got these things cleared away, and my housekeeping done.'

I pressed my services upon him, somewhat feebly, I own, for I can't bear dishwater; but he rejected my offer.

'I don't like trusting my china to the hands of a tender-foot.'

'Quite right, though your china would prove an excellent means of defence at long range.' It was delf, a quarter of an inch thick. So I smoked while he washed up, swept, dusted, and arranged the room.

After the room was ordered to his taste, we proceeded to hold council. He could offer dinner, magic lantern, music. 'We can fill in time for two hours, but,' he added gloomily, 'we can't beat the dance and the "High Kickers."'

'Have you nothing new or startling?'

He shook his head.

'No kind of show? Dog show? Snake charmer?'

'Slavin has a monopoly of the snakes.'

Then he added hesitatingly, 'There was an old Punch-and-Judy chap here last year, but he died. Whisky again.'

'What happened to his show?'

'The Black Rock Hotel man took it for board and whisky bill. He has it still, I suppose.'

I did not much relish the business; but I hated to see him beaten, so I ventured, 'I have run a Punch and Judy in an amateur way at the 'Varsity.'

He sprang to his feet with a yell.

'You have! you mean to say it? We've got them! We've beaten them!' He had an extraordinary way of taking your help for granted. 'The miner chaps, mostly English and Welsh, went mad over the poor old showman, and made him so wealthy that in sheer gratitude he drank himself to death.'

He walked up and down in high excitement and in such evident delight that I felt pledged to my best effort.

'Well,' I said, 'first the poster. We must beat them in that.'

He brought me large sheets of brown paper, and after two hours' hard work I had half a dozen pictorial showbills done in gorgeous colours and striking designs. They were good, if I do say it myself.

The turkey, the magic lantern, the Punch and Judy show were all there, the last with a crowd before it in gaping delight. A few explanatory words were thrown in, emphasising the highly artistic nature of the Punch and Judy entertainment.

Craig was delighted, and proceeded to perfect his plans. He had some half a dozen young men, four young ladies, and eight or ten matrons, upon whom he could depend for help. These he organised into a vigilance committee charged with the duty of preventing miners and lumbermen from getting away to Slavin's. 'The critical moments will be immediately before and after dinner, and then again after the show is over,' he explained. 'The first two crises must be left to the care of Punch and Judy, and as for the last, I am not yet sure what shall be done'; but I saw he had something in his head, for he added, 'I shall see Mrs. Mavor.'

'Who is Mrs. Mavor?' I asked. But he made no reply. He was a born fighter, and he put the fighting spirit into us all. We were bound to win.

The sports were to begin at two o'clock. By lunch-time everything was in readiness. After lunch I was having a quiet smoke in Craig's shack when in he rushed, saying--

'The battle will be lost before it is fought. If we lose Quatre Bras, we shall never get to Waterloo.'

'What's up?'

'Slavin, just now. The miners are coming in, and he will have them in tow in half an hour.'

He looked at me appealingly. I knew what he wanted.

'All right; I suppose I must, but it is an awful bore that a man can't have a quiet smoke.'

'You're not half a bad fellow,' he replied, smiling. 'I shall get the ladies to furnish coffee inside the booth. You furnish them intellectual nourishment in front with dear old Punch and Judy.'

He sent a boy with a bell round the village announcing, 'Punch, and Judy in front of the Christmas booth beside the church'; and for three-quarters of an hour I shrieked and sweated in that awful little pen. But it was almost worth it to hear the shouts of approval and laughter that greeted my performance. It was cold work standing about, so that the crowd was quite ready to respond when Punch, after being duly hanged, came forward and invited all into the booth for the hot coffee which Judy had ordered.

In they trooped, and Quatre Bras was won.

No sooner were the miners safely engaged with their coffee than I heard a great noise of bells and of men shouting; and on reaching the street I saw that the men from the lumber camp were coming in. Two immense sleighs, decorated with ribbons and spruce boughs, each drawn by a four-horse team gaily adorned, filled with some fifty men, singing and shouting with all their might, were coming down the hill road at full gallop. Round the corner they swung, dashed at full speed across the bridge and down the street, and pulled up after they had made the circuit of a block, to the great admiration of the onlookers. Among others Slavin sauntered up good-naturedly, making himself agreeable to Sandy and those who were helping to unhitch his team.

'Oh, you need not take trouble with me or my team, Mike Slavin. Batchees and me and the boys can look after them fine,' said Sandy coolly.

This rejecting of hospitality was perfectly understood by Slavin and by all.

'Dat's too bad, heh?' said Baptiste wickedly; 'and, Sandy, he's got good money on his pocket for sure, too.' The boys laughed, and Slavin, joining in, turned away with Keele and Blaney; but by the look in his eye I knew he was playing 'Br'er Rabbit,' and lying low.

Mr. Craig just then came up, 'Hello, boys! too late for Punch and Judy, but just in time for hot coffee and doughnuts.'

'Bon; dat's fuss rate,' said Baptiste heartily; 'where you keep him?'

'Up in the tent next the church there. The miners are all in.'

'Ah, dat so? Dat's bad news for the shantymen, heh, Sandy?' said the little Frenchman dolefully.

'There was a clothes-basket full of doughnuts and a boiler of coffee left as I passed just now,' said Craig encouragingly.

'Allons, mes garcons; vite! never say keel!' cried Baptiste excitedly, stripping off the harness.

But Sandy would not leave the horses till they were carefully rubbed down, blanketed, and fed, for he was entered for the four-horse race and it behoved him to do his best to win. Besides, he scorned to hurry himself for anything so unimportant as eating; that he considered hardly worthy even of Baptiste. Mr. Craig managed to get a word with him before he went off, and I saw Sandy solemnly and emphatically shake his head, saying, 'Ah! we'll beat him this day,' and I gathered that he was added to the vigilance committee.

Old man Nelson was busy with his own team. He turned slowly at Mr. Craig's greeting, 'How is it, Nelson?' and it was with a very grave voice he answered, 'I hardly know, sir; but I am not gone yet, though it seems little to hold to.'

'All you want for a grip is what your hand can cover. What would you have? And besides, do you know why you are not gone yet?'

The old man waited, looking at the minister gravely.

'Because He hasn't let go His grip of you.'

'How do you know He's gripped me?'

'Now, look here, Nelson, do you want to quit this thing and give it all up?'

'No, no! For heaven's sake, no! Why, do you think I have lost it?' said Nelson, almost piteously.

'Well, He's keener about it than you; and I'll bet you haven't thought it worth while to thank Him.'

'To thank Him,' he repeated, almost stupidly, 'for--'

'For keeping you where you are overnight,' said Mr. Craig, almost sternly.

The old man gazed at the minister, a light growing in his eyes.

'You're right. Thank God, you're right.' And then he turned quickly away, and went into the stable behind his team. It was a minute before he came out. Over his face there was a trembling joy.

'Can I do anything for you to-day?' he asked humbly.

'Indeed you just can,' said the minister, taking his hand and shaking it very warmly; and then he told him Slavin's programme and ours.

'Sandy is all right till after his race. After that is his time of danger,' said the minister.

'I'll stay with him, sir,' said old Nelson, in the tone of a man taking a covenant, and immediately set off for the coffee-tent.

'Here comes another recruit for your corps,' I said, pointing to Leslie Graeme, who was coming down the street at that moment in his light sleigh.

'I am not so sure. Do you think you could get him?'

I laughed. 'You are a good one.'

'Well,' he replied, half defiantly, 'is not this your fight too?'

'You make me think so, though I am bound to say I hardly recognise myself to day. But here goes,' and before I knew it I was describing our plans to Graeme, growing more and more enthusiastic as he sat in his sleigh, listening with a quizzical smile I didn't quite like.

'He's got you too,' he said; 'I feared so.'

'Well,' I laughed, 'perhaps so. But I want to lick that man Slavin. I've just seen him, and he's just what Craig calls him, "a slick son of the devil." Don't be shocked; he says it is Scripture.'

'Revised version,' said Graeme gravely, while Craig looked a little abashed.

'What is assigned me, Mr. Craig? for I know that this man is simply your agent.'

I repudiated the idea, while Mr. Craig said nothing.

'What's my part?' demanded Graeme.

'Well,' said Mr. Craig hesitatingly, 'of course I would do nothing till I had consulted you; but I want a man to take my place at the sports. I am referee.'

'That's all right,' said Graeme, with an air of relief; 'I expected something hard.'

'And then I thought you would not mind presiding at dinner--I want it to go off well.'

'Did you notice that?' said Graeme to me. 'Not a bad touch, eh?'

'That's nothing to the way he touched me. Wait and learn,' I answered, while Craig looked quite distressed. 'He'll do it, Mr. Craig, never fear,' I said, 'and any other little duty that may occur to you.'

'Now that's too bad of you. That is all I want, honour bright,' he replied; adding, as he turned away, 'you are just in time for a cup of coffee, Mr. Graeme. Now I must see Mrs. Mavor.'

'Who is Mrs. Mavor?' I demanded of Graeme.

'Mrs. Mavor? The miners' guardian angel.'

We put up the horses and set off for coffee. As we approached the booth Graeme caught sight of the Punch and Judy show, stood still in amazement, and exclaimed, 'Can the dead live?'

'Punch and Judy never die,' I replied solemnly.

'But the old manipulator is dead enough, poor old beggar!'

'But he left his mantle, as you see.'

He looked at me a moment

'What! do you mean, you--?'

'Yes, that is exactly what I do mean.'

'He is great man, that Craig fellow--a truly great man.'

And then he leaned up against a tree and laughed till the tears came. 'I say, old boy, don't mind me,' he gasped, 'but do you remember the old 'Varsity show?'

'Yes, you villain; and I remember your part in it. I wonder how you can, even at this remote date, laugh at it.' For I had a vivid recollection of how, after a 'chaste and highly artistic performance of this mediaeval play' had been given before a distinguished Toronto audience, the trap door by which I had entered my box was fastened, and I was left to swelter in my cage, and forced to listen to the suffocated laughter from the wings and the stage whispers of 'Hello, Mr. Punch, where's the baby?' And for many a day after I was subjected to anxious inquiries as to the locality and health of 'the baby,' and whether it was able to be out.

'Oh, the dear old days!' he kept saying, over and over, in a tone so full of sadness that my heart grew sore for him and I forgave him, as many a time before.

The sports passed off in typical Western style. In addition to the usual running and leaping contests, there was rifle and pistol shooting, in both of which old man Nelson stood first, with Shaw, foreman of the mines, second.

The great event of the day, however, was to be the four-horse race, for which three teams were entered--one from the mines driven by Nixon, Craig's friend, a citizens' team, and Sandy's. The race was really between the miners' team, and that from the woods, for the citizens' team, though made up of speedy horses, had not been driven much together, and knew neither their driver nor each other. In the miners' team were four bays, very powerful, a trifle heavy perhaps, but well matched, perfectly trained, and perfectly handled by their driver. Sandy had his long rangy roans, and for leaders a pair of half-broken pinto bronchos. The pintos, caught the summer before upon the Alberta prairies, were fleet as deer, but wicked and uncertain. They were Baptiste's special care and pride. If they would only run straight there was little doubt that they would carry the roans and themselves to glory; but one could not tell the moment they might bolt or kick things to pieces.

Being the only non-partisan in the crowd I was asked to referee. The race was about half a mile and return, the first and last quarters being upon the ice. The course, after leaving the ice, led up from the river by a long easy slope to the level above; and at the further end curved somewhat sharply round the Old Fort. The only condition attaching to the race was that the teams should start from the scratch, make the turn of the Fort, and finish at the scratch. There were no vexing regulations as to fouls. The man making the foul would find it necessary to reckon with the crowd, which was considered sufficient guarantee for a fair and square race. Owing to the hazards of the course, the result would depend upon the skill of the drivers quite as much as upon the speed of the teams. The points of hazard were at the turn round the Old Fort, and at a little ravine which led down to the river, over which the road passed by means of a long log bridge or causeway.

From a point upon the high bank of the river the whole course lay in open view. It was a scene full of life and vividly picturesque. There were miners in dark clothes and peak caps; citizens in ordinary garb; ranchmen in wide cowboy hats and buckskin shirts and leggings, some with cartridge-belts and pistols; a few half-breeds and Indians in half-native, half-civilised dress; and scattering through the crowd the lumbermen with gay scarlet and blue blanket coats, and some with knitted tuques of the same colours. A very good-natured but extremely uncertain crowd it was. At the head of each horse stood a man, but at the pintos' heads Baptiste stood alone, trying to hold down the off leader, thrown into a frenzy of fear by the yelling of the crowd.

Gradually all became quiet, till, in the midst of absolute stillness, came the words, 'Are you ready?', then the pistol-shot and the great race had begun. Above the roar of the crowd came the shrill cry of Baptiste, as he struck his broncho with the palm of his hand, and swung himself into the sleigh beside Sandy, as it shot past.

Like a flash the bronchos sprang to the front, two lengths before the other teams; but, terrified by the yelling of the crowd, instead of bending to the left bank up which the road wound, they wheeled to the right and were almost across the river before Sandy could swing them back into the course.

Baptiste's cries, a curious mixture of French and English, continued to strike through all other sounds till they gained the top of the slope to find the others almost a hundred yards in front, the citizens' team leading, with the miners' following close. The moment the pintos caught sight of the teams before them they set off at a terrific pace and steadily devoured the intervening space. Nearer and nearer the turn came, the eight horses in front, running straight and well within their speed. After them flew the pintos, running savagely with ears set back, leading well the big roans, thundering along and gaining at every bound. And now the citizens' team had almost reached the Fort, running hard, and drawing away from the bays. But Nixon knew what he was about, and was simply steadying his team for the turn. The event proved his wisdom, for in the turn the leading team left the track, lost a moment or two in the deep snow, and before they could regain the road the bays had swept superbly past, leaving their rivals to follow in the rear. On came the pintos, swiftly nearing the Fort. Surely at that pace they cannot make the turn. But Sandy knows his leaders. They have their eyes upon the teams in front, and need no touch of rein. Without the slightest change in speed the nimble-footed bronchos round the turn, hauling the big roans after them, and fall in behind the citizens' team, which is regaining steadily the ground lost in the turn.

And now the struggle is for the bridge over the ravine. The bays in front, running with mouths wide open, are evidently doing their best; behind them, and every moment nearing them, but at the limit of their speed too, come the lighter and fleeter citizens' team; while opposite their driver are the pintos, pulling hard, eager and fresh. Their temper is too uncertain to send them to the front; they run well following, but when leading cannot be trusted, and besides, a broncho hates a bridge; so Sandy holds them where they are, waiting and hoping for his chance after the bridge is crossed. Foot by foot the citizens' team creep up upon the flank of the bays, with the pintos in turn hugging them closely, till it seems as if the three, if none slackens, must strike the bridge together; and this will mean destruction to one at least. This danger Sandy perceives, but he dare not check his leaders. Suddenly, within a few yards of the bridge, Baptiste throws himself upon the lines, wrenches them out of Sandy's hands, and, with a quick swing, faces the pintos down the steep side of the ravine, which is almost sheer ice with a thin coat of snow. It is a daring course to take, for the ravine, though not deep, is full of undergrowth, and is partially closed up by a brush heap at the further end. But, with a yell, Baptiste hurls his four horses down the slope, and into the undergrowth. 'Allons, mes enfants! Courage! vite, vite!' cries their driver, and nobly do the pintos respond. Regardless of bushes and brush heaps, they tear their way through; but, as they emerge, the hind bob-sleigh catches a root, and, with a crash, the sleigh is hurled high in the air. Baptiste's cries ring out high and shrill as ever, encouraging his team, and never cease till, with a plunge and a scramble, they clear the brush heap lying at the mouth of the ravine, and are out on the ice on the river, with Baptiste standing on the front bob, the box trailing behind, and Sandy nowhere to be seen.

Three hundred yards of the course remain. The bays, perfectly handled, have gained at the bridge and in the descent to the ice, and are leading the citizens' team by half a dozen sleigh lengths. Behind both comes Baptiste. It is now or never for the pintos. The rattle of the trailing box, together with the wild yelling of the crowd rushing down the bank, excites the bronchos to madness, and, taking the bits in their teeth, they do their first free running that day. Past the citizens' team like a whirlwind they dash, clear the intervening space, and gain the flanks of the bays. Can the bays hold them? Over them leans their driver, plying for the first time the hissing lash. Only fifty yards more. The miners begin to yell. But Baptiste, waving his lines high in one hand seizes his tuque with the other, whirls it about his head and flings it with a fiercer yell than ever at the bronchos. Like the bursting of a hurricane the pintos leap forward, and with a splendid rush cross the scratch, winners by their own length.

There was a wild quarter of an hour. The shantymen had torn off their coats and were waving them wildly and tossing them high, while the ranchers added to the uproar by emptying their revolvers into the air in a way that made one nervous.

When the crowd was somewhat quieted Sandy's stiff figure appeared, slowly making towards them. A dozen lumbermen ran to him, eagerly inquiring if he were hurt. But Sandy could only curse the little Frenchman for losing the race.

'Lost! Why, man, we've won it!' shouted a voice, at which Sandy's rage vanished, and he allowed himself to be carried in upon the shoulders of his admirers.

'Where's the lad?' was his first question.

'The bronchos are off with him. He's down at the rapids like enough.'

'Let me go,' shouted Sandy, setting off at a run in the track of the sleigh. He had not gone far before he met Baptiste coming back with his team foaming, the roans going quietly, but the bronchos dancing, and eager to be at it again.

'Voila! bully boy! tank the bon Dieu, Sandy; you not keel, heh? Ah! you are one grand chevalier,' exclaimed Baptiste, hauling Sandy in and thrusting the lines into his hands. And so they came back, the sleigh box still dragging behind, the pintos executing fantastic figures on their hind legs, and Sandy holding them down. The little Frenchman struck a dramatic attitude and called out--

'Voila! What's the matter wiz Sandy, heh?'

The roar that answered set the bronchos off again plunging and kicking, and only when Baptiste got them by the heads could they be induced to stand long enough to allow Sandy to be proclaimed winner of the race. Several of the lumbermen sprang into the sleigh box with Sandy and Baptiste, among them Keefe, followed by Nelson, and the first part of the great day was over. Slavin could not understand the new order of things. That a great event like the four-horse race should not be followed by 'drinks all round' was to him at once disgusting and incomprehensible; and, realising his defeat for the moment, he fell into the crowd and disappeared. But he left behind him his 'runners.' He had not yet thrown up the game.

Mr. Craig meantime came to me, and, looking anxiously after Sandy in his sleigh, with his frantic crowd of yelling admirers, said in a gloomy voice, 'Poor Sandy! He is easily caught, and Keefe has the devil's cunning.'

'He won't touch Slavin's whisky to-day,' I answered confidently.

'There'll be twenty bottles waiting him in the stable,' he replied bitterly, 'and I can't go following him up.'

'He won't stand that, no man would. God help us all.' I could hardly recognise myself, for I found in my heart an earnest echo to that prayer as I watched him go toward the crowd again, his face set in strong determination. He looked like the captain of a forlorn hope, and I was proud to be following him.

CHAPTER III
WATERLOO. OUR FIGHT--HIS VICTORY

The sports were over, and there remained still an hour to be filled in before dinner. It was an hour full of danger to Craig's hopes of victory, for the men were wild with excitement, and ready for the most reckless means of 'slinging their dust.' I could not but admire the skill with which Mr. Craig caught their attention.

'Gentlemen,' he called out, 'we've forgotten the judge of the great race. Three cheers for Mr. Connor!'

Two of the shantymen picked me up and hoisted me on their shoulders while the cheers were given.

'Announce the Punch and Judy,' he entreated me, in a low voice. I did so in a little speech, and was forthwith borne aloft, through the street to the booth, followed by the whole crowd, cheering like mad.

The excitement of the crowd caught me, and for an hour I squeaked and worked the wires of the immortal and unhappy family in a manner hitherto unapproached by me at least. I was glad enough when Graeme came to tell me to send the men in to dinner. This Mr. Punch did in the most gracious manner, and again with cheers for Punch's master they trooped tumultuously into the tent.

We had only well begun when Baptiste came in quietly but hurriedly and whispered to me--

'M'sieu Craig, he's gone to Slavin's, and would lak you and M'sieu Graeme would follow queek. Sandy he's take one leel drink up at de stable, and he's go mad lak one diable.'

I sent him for Graeme, who was presiding at dinner, and set off for Slavin's at a run. There I found Mr. Craig and Nelson holding Sandy, more than half drunk, back from Slavin, who, stripped to the shirt, was coolly waiting with a taunting smile.

'Let me go, Mr. Craig,' Sandy was saying, 'I am a good Presbyterian. He is a Papist thief; and he has my money; and I will have it out of the soul of him.'

'Let him go, preacher,' sneered Slavin, 'I'll cool him off for yez. But ye'd better hold him if yez wants his mug left on to him.'

'Let him go!' Keefe was shouting.

'Hands off!' Blaney was echoing.

I pushed my way in. 'What's up?' I cried.

'Mr. Connor,' said Sandy solemnly, 'it is a gentleman you are, though your name is against you, and I am a good Presbyterian, and I can give you the Commandments and Reasons annexed to them; but yon's a thief, a Papist thief, and I am justified in getting my money out of his soul.'

'But,' I remonstrated, 'you won't get it in this way.'

'He has my money,' reiterated Sandy.

'He is a blank liar, and he's afraid to take it up,' said Slavin, in a low, cool tone.

With a roar Sandy broke away and rushed at him; but, without moving from his tracks, Slavin met him with a straight left-hander and laid him flat.

'Hooray,' yelled Blaney, 'Ireland for ever!' and, seizing the iron poker, swung it around his head, crying, 'Back, or, by the holy Moses, I'll kill the first man that interferes wid the game.'

'Give it to him!' Keefe said savagely.

Sandy rose slowly, gazing round stupidly.

'He don't know what hit him,' laughed Keefe.

This roused the Highlander, and saying, 'I'll settle you afterwards, Mister Keefe,' he rushed in again at Slavin. Again Slavin met him again with his left, staggered him, and, before he fell, took a step forward and delivered a terrific right-hand blow on his jaw. Poor Sandy went down in a heap amid the yells of Blaney, Keefe, and some others of the gang. I was in despair when in came Baptiste and Graeme.

One look at Sandy, and Baptiste tore off his coat and cap, slammed them on the floor, danced on them, and with a long-drawn 'sap-r-r-rie,' rushed at Slavin. But Graeme caught him by the back of the neck, saying, 'Hold on, little man,' and turning to Slavin, pointed to Sandy, who was reviving under Nelson's care, and said, 'What's this for?'

'Ask him,' said Slavin insolently. 'He knows.'

'What is it, Nelson?'

Nelson explained that Sandy, after drinking some at the stable and a glass at the Black Rock Hotel, had come down here with Keefe and the others, had lost his money, and was accusing Slavin of robbing him.

'Did you furnish him with liquor?' said Graeme sternly.

'It is none of your business,' replied Slavin, with an oath.

'I shall make it my business. It is not the first time my men have lost money in this saloon.'

'You lie,' said Slavin, with deliberate emphasis.

'Slavin,' said Graeme quietly, 'it's a pity you said that, because, unless you apologise in one minute, I shall make you sorry.'

'Apologise?' roared Slavin, 'apologise to you?' calling him a vile name.

Graeme grew white, and said even more slowly, 'Now you'll have to take it; no apology will do.'

He slowly stripped off coat and vest. Mr. Craig interposed, begging Graeme to let the matter pass. 'Surely he is not worth it.'

'Mr. Craig,' said Graeme, with an easy smile, 'you don't understand. No man can call me that name and walk around afterwards feeling well.'

Then, turning to Slavin, he said, 'Now, if you want a minute's rest, I can wait.'

Slavin, with a curse, bade him come.

'Blaney,' said Graeme sharply, 'you get back.' Blaney promptly stepped back to Keefe's side. 'Nelson, you and Baptiste can see that they stay there.' The old man nodded and looked at Craig, who simply said, 'Do the best you can.'

It was a good fight. Slavin had plenty of pluck, and for a time forced the fighting, Graeme guarding easily and tapping him aggravatingly about the nose and eyes, drawing blood, but not disabling him. Gradually there came a look of fear into Slavin's eyes, and the beads stood upon his face. He had met his master.

'Now, Slavin, you're beginning to be sorry; and now I am going to show you what you are made of.' Graeme made one or two lightning passes, struck Slavin one, two, three terrific blows, and laid him quite flat and senseless. Keefe and Blaney both sprang forward, but there was a savage kind of growl.

'Hold, there!' It was old man Nelson looking along a pistol barrel. 'You know me, Keefe,' he said. 'You won't do any murder this time.'

Keefe turned green and yellow, and staggered back, while Slavin slowly rose to his feet.

'Will you take some more?' said Graeme. 'You haven't got much; but mind I have stopped playing with you. Put up your gun, Nelson. No one will interfere now.'

Slavin hesitated, then rushed, but Graeme stepped to meet him, and we saw Slavin's heels in the air as he fell back upon his neck and shoulders and lay still, with his toes quivering.

'Bon!' yelled Baptiste. 'Bully boy! Dat's de bon stuff. Dat's larn him one good lesson.' But immediately he shrieked, Gar-r-r-e a vous!'

He was too late, for there was a crash of breaking glass, and Graeme fell to the floor with a long deep cut on the side of his head. Keefe had hurled a bottle with all too sure an aim, and had fled. I thought he was dead; but we carried him out, and in a few minutes he groaned, opened his eyes, and sank again into insensibility.

'Where can we take him?' I cried.

'To my shack,' said Mr. Craig.

'Is there no place nearer?'

'Yes; Mrs. Mavor's. I shall run on to tell her.'

She met us at the door. I had in mind to say some words of apology, but when I looked upon her face I forgot my words, forgot my business at her door, and stood simply looking.

'Come in! Bring him in! Please do not wait,' she said, and her voice was sweet and soft and firm.

We laid him in a large room at the back of the shop over which Mrs. Mavor lived. Together we dressed the wound, her firm white fingers, skilful as if with long training. Before the dressing was finished I sent Craig off, for the time had come for the Magic Lantern in the church, and I knew how critical the moment was in our fight. 'Go,' I said; 'he is coming to, and we do not need you.'

In a few moments more Graeme revived, and, gazing about, asked, 'What's, all this about?' and then, recollecting, 'Ah! that brute Keefe'; then seeing my anxious face he said carelessly, 'Awful bore, ain't it? Sorry to trouble you, old fellow.'

'You be hanged!' I said shortly; for his old sweet smile was playing about his lips, and was almost too much for me. 'Mrs. Mavor and I are in command, and you must keep perfectly still.'

'Mrs. Mavor?' he said, in surprise. She came forward, with a slight flush on her face.

'I think you know me, Mr. Graeme.'

'I have often seen you, and wished to know you. I am sorry to bring you this trouble.'

'You must not say so,' she replied, 'but let me do all for you that I can. And now the doctor says you are to lie still.'

'The doctor? Oh! you mean Connor. He is hardly there yet. You don't know each other. Permit me to present Mr. Connor, Mrs. Mavor.'

As she bowed slightly, her eyes looked into mine with serious gaze, not inquiring, yet searching my soul. As I looked into her eyes I forgot everything about me, and when I recalled myself it seemed as if I had been away in some far place. It was not their colour or their brightness; I do not yet know their colour, and I have often looked into them; and they were not bright; but they were clear, and one could look far down into them, and in their depths see a glowing, steady light. As I went to get some drugs from the Black Rock doctor, I found myself wondering about that far-down light; and about her voice, how it could get that sound from far away.

I found the doctor quite drunk, as indeed Mr. Craig had warned; but his drugs were good, and I got what I wanted and quickly returned.

While Graeme slept Mrs. Mavor made me tea. As the evening wore on I told her the events of the day, dwelling admiringly upon Craig's generalship. She smiled at this.

'He got me too,' she said. 'Nixon was sent to me just before the sports; and I don't think he will break down to-day, and I am so thankful.' And her eyes glowed.

'I am quite sure he won't,' I thought to myself, but I said no word.

After a long pause, she went on, 'I have promised Mr. Craig to sing to-night, if I am needed!' and then, after a moment's hesitation, 'It is two years since I have been able to sing--two years,' she repeated, 'since'--and then her brave voice trembled--'my husband was killed.'

'I quite understand,' I said, having no other word on my tongue

'And,' she went on quietly, 'I fear I have been selfish. It is hard to sing the same songs. We were very happy. But the miners like to hear me sing, and I think perhaps it helps them to feel less lonely, and keeps them from evil. I shall try to-night, if I am needed. Mr. Craig will not ask me unless he must.'

I would have seen every miner and lumberman in the place hideously drunk before I would have asked her to sing one song while her heart ached. I wondered at Craig, and said, rather angrily--

'He thinks only of those wretched miners and shantymen of his.'

She looked at me with wonder in her eyes, and said gently, 'And are they not Christ's too?'

And I found no word to reply.

It was nearing ten o'clock, and I was wondering how the fight was going, and hoping that Mrs. Mavor would not be needed, when the door opened, and old man Nelson and Sandy, the latter much battered and ashamed, came in with the word for Mrs. Mavor.

'I will come,' she said simply. She saw me preparing to accompany her, and asked, 'Do you think you can leave him?'

'He will do quite well in Nelson's care.'

'Then I am glad; for I must take my little one with me. I did not put her to bed in case I should need to go, and I may not leave her.'

We entered the church by the back door, and saw at once that even yet the battle might easily be lost.

Some miners had just come from Slavin's, evidently bent on breaking up the meeting, in revenge for the collapse of the dance, which Slavin was unable to enjoy, much less direct. Craig was gallantly holding his ground, finding it hard work to keep his men in good humour, and so prevent a fight, for there were cries of 'Put him out! Put the beast out!' at a miner half drunk and wholly outrageous.

The look of relief that came over his face when Craig caught sight of us told how anxious he had been, and reconciled me to Mrs. Mavor's singing. 'Thank the good God,' he said, with what came near being a sob, 'I was about to despair.'

He immediately walked to the front and called out--

'Gentlemen, if you wish it, Mrs. Mavor will sing.'

There was a dead silence. Some one began to applaud, but a miner said savagely, 'Stop that, you fool!'

There was a few moments' delay, when from the crowd a voice called out, 'Does Mrs. Mavor wish to sing?' followed by cries of 'Ay, that's it.' Then Shaw, the foreman at the mines, stood up in the audience and said--

'Mr. Craig and gentlemen, you know that three years ago I was known as "Old Ricketts," and that I owe all I am to-night, under God, to Mrs. Mavor, and'--with a little quiver in his voice--'her baby. And we all know that for two years she has not sung; and we all know why. And what I say is, that if she does not feel like singing to-night, she is not going to sing to keep any drunken brute of Slavin's crowd quiet.'

There were deep growls of approval all over the church. I could have hugged Shaw then and there. Mr. Craig went to Mrs. Mavor, and after a word with her came back and said--

'Mrs. Mavor, wishes me to thank her dear friend Mr. Shaw, but says she would like to sing.'

The response was perfect stillness. Mr. Craig sat down to the organ and played the opening bars of the touching melody, 'Oft in the Stilly Night.' Mrs. Mavor came to the front, and, with a smile of exquisite sweetness upon her sad face, and looking straight at us with her glorious eyes, began to sing.

Her voice, a rich soprano, even and true, rose and fell, now soft, now strong, but always filling the building, pouring around us floods of music. I had heard Patti's 'Home, sweet Home,' and of all singing that alone affected me as did this.

At the end of the first verse the few women in the church and some men were weeping quietly; but when she began the words--

'When I remember all
The friends once linked together,'

sobs came on every side from these tender-hearted fellows, and Shaw quite lost his grip. But she sang steadily on, the tone clearer and sweeter and fuller at every note, and when the sound of her voice died away, she stood looking at the men as if in wonder that they should weep. No one moved. Mr. Craig played softly on, and, wandering through many variations, arrived at last at

'Jesus, lover of my soul.'

As she sang the appealing words, her face was lifted up, and she saw none of us; but she must have seen some one, for the cry in her voice could only come from one who could see and feel help close at hand. On and on went the glorious voice, searching my soul's depths; but when she came to the words--

'Thou, O Christ, art all I want,'

she stretched up her arms--she had quite forgotten us, her voice had borne her to other worlds--and sang with such a passion of 'abandon' that my soul was ready to surrender anything, everything.

Again Mr. Craig wandered on through his changing chords till again he came to familiar ground, and the voice began, in low, thrilling tones, Bernard's great song of home--

'Jerusalem the golden.'

Every word, with all its weight of meaning, came winging to our souls, till we found ourselves gazing afar into those stately halls of Zion, with their daylight serene and their jubilant throngs. When the singer came to the last verse there was a pause. Again Mr. Craig softly played the interlude, but still there was no voice. I looked up. She was very white, and her eyes were glowing with their deep light. Mr. Craig looked quickly about, saw her, stopped, and half rose, as if to go to her, when, in a voice that seemed to come from a far-off land, she went on--

'O sweet and blessed country!'

The longing, the yearning, in the second 'O' were indescribable. Again and again, as she held that word, and then dropped down with the cadence in the music, my heart ached for I knew not what.

The audience were sitting as in a trance. The grimy faces of the miners, for they never get quite white, were furrowed with the tear-courses. Shaw, by this time, had his face too lifted high, his eyes gazing far above the singer's head, and I knew by the rapture in his face that he was seeing, as she saw, the thronging stately halls and the white-robed conquerors. He had felt, and was still feeling, all the stress of the fight, and to him the vision of the conquerors in their glory was soul-drawing and soul-stirring. And Nixon, too--he had his vision; but what he saw was the face of the singer, with the shining eyes, and, by the look of him, that was vision enough.

Immediately after her last note Mrs. Mavor stretched out her hands to her little girl, who was sitting on my knee, caught her up, and, holding her close to her breast, walked quickly behind the curtain. Not a sound followed the singing: no one moved till she had disappeared; and then Mr. Craig came to the front, and, motioning to me to follow Mrs. Mavor, began in a low, distinct voice--

'Gentlemen, it was not easy for Mrs. Mavor to sing for us, and you know she sang because she is a miner's wife, and her heart is with the miners. But she sang, too, because her heart is His who came to earth this day so many years ago to save us all; and she would make you love Him too. For in loving Him you are saved from all base loves, and you know what I mean.

'And before we say good-night, men, I want to know if the time is not come when all of you who mean to be better than you are should join in putting from us this thing that has brought sorrow and shame to us and to those we love? You know what I mean. Some of you are strong; will you stand by and see weaker men robbed of the money they save for those far away, and robbed of the manhood that no money can buy or restore?

'Will the strong men help? Shall we all join hands in this? What do you say? In this town we have often seen hell, and just a moment ago we were all looking into heaven, "the sweet and blessed country." O men!' and his voice rang in an agony through the building--'O men! which shall be ours? For Heaven's dear sake, let us help one another! Who will?'

I was looking out through a slit in the curtain. The men, already wrought to intense feeling by the music, were listening with set faces and gleaming eyes, and as at the appeal 'Who will?' Craig raised high his hand, Shaw, Nixon, and a hundred men sprang to their feet and held high their hands.

I have witnessed some thrilling scenes in my life, but never anything to equal that: the one man on the platform standing at full height, with his hand thrown up to heaven, and the hundred men below standing straight, with arms up at full length, silent, and almost motionless.

For a moment Craig held them so; and again his voice rang out, louder, sterner than before--

'All who mean it, say, "By God's help I will."' And back from a hundred throats came deep and strong the words, 'By God's help, I will.'

At this point Mrs. Mavor, whom I had quite forgotten, put her hand on my arm. 'Go and tell him,' she panted, 'I want them to come on Thursday night, as they used to in the other days--go--quick,' and she almost pushed me out. I gave Craig her message. He held up his hand for silence.

'Mrs. Mavor wishes me to say that she will be glad to see you all, as in the old days, on Thursday evening; and I can think of no better place to give formal expression to our pledge of this night'

There was a shout of acceptance; and then, at some one's call, the long pent-up feelings of the crowd found vent in three mighty cheers for Mrs. Mavor.

'Now for our old hymn,' called out Mr. Craig, 'and Mrs. Mavor will lead us.'

He sat down at the organ, played a few bars of 'The Sweet By and By,' and then Mrs. Mavor began. But not a soul joined till the refrain was reached, and then they sang as only men with their hearts on fire can sing. But after the last refrain Mr.

Craig made a sign to Mrs. Mavor, and she sang alone, slowly and softly, and with eyes looking far away--

'In the sweet by and by,   We shall meet on that beautiful shore.'

There was no benediction--there seemed no need; and the men went quietly out. But over and over again the voice kept singing in my ears and in my heart, 'We shall meet on that beautiful shore.' And after the sleigh-loads of men had gone and left the street empty, as I stood with Craig in the radiant moonlight that made the great mountains about come near us, from Sandy's sleigh we heard in the distance Baptiste's French-English song; but the song that floated down with the sound of the bells from the miners' sleigh was--

'We shall meet on that beautiful shore.'

'Poor old Shaw!' said Craig softly.

When the last sound had died away I turned to him and said--

'You have won your fight.'

'We have won our fight; I was beaten,' he replied quickly, offering me his hand. Then, taking off his cap, and looking up beyond the mountain-tops and the silent stars, he added softly, 'Our fight, but His victory.'

And, thinking it all over, I could not say but perhaps he was right.

CHAPTER IV
MRS. MAVOR'S STORY

The days that followed the Black Rock Christmas were anxious days and weary, but not for the brightest of my life would I change them now; for, as after the burning heat or rocking storm the dying day lies beautiful in the tender glow of the evening, so these days have lost their weariness and lie bathed in a misty glory. The years that bring us many ills, and that pass so stormfully over us, bear away with them the ugliness, the weariness, the pain that are theirs, but the beauty, the sweetness, the rest they leave untouched, for these are eternal. As the mountains, that near at hand stand jagged and scarred, in the far distance repose in their soft robes of purple haze, so the rough present fades into the past, soft and sweet and beautiful.

I have set myself to recall the pain and anxiety of those days and nights when we waited in fear for the turn of the fever, but I can only think of the patience and gentleness and courage of her who stood beside me, bearing more than half my burden. And while I can see the face of Leslie Graeme, ghastly or flushed, and hear his low moaning or the broken words of his delirium, I think chiefly of the bright face bending over him, and of the cool, firm, swift-moving hands that soothed and smoothed and rested, and the voice, like the soft song of a bird in the twilight, that never failed to bring peace.

Mrs. Mavor and I were much together during those days. I made my home in Mr. Craig's shack, but most of my time was spent beside my friend. We did not see much of Craig, for he was heart-deep with the miners, laying plans for the making of the League the following Thursday; and though he shared our anxiety and was ever ready to relieve us, his thought and his talk had mostly to do with the League.

Mrs. Mavor's evenings were given to the miners, but her afternoons mostly to Graeme and to me, and then it was I saw another side of her character. We would sit in her little dining-room, where the pictures on the walls, the quaint old silver, and bits of curiously cut glass, all spoke of other and different days, and thence we would roam the world of literature and art. Keenly sensitive to all the good and beautiful in these, she had her favourites among the masters, for whom she was ready to do battle; and when her argument, instinct with fancy and vivid imagination, failed, she swept away all opposing opinion with the swift rush of her enthusiasm; so that, though I felt she was beaten, I was left without words to reply. Shakespeare and Tennyson and Burns she loved, but not Shelley, nor Byron, nor even Wordsworth. Browning she knew not, and therefore could not rank him with her noblest three; but when I read to her 'A Death in the Desert,' and, came to the noble words at the end of the tale--

'For all was as I say, and now the man
Lies as he once lay, breast to breast with God,'

the light shone in her eyes, and she said, 'Oh, that is good and great; I shall get much out of him; I had always feared he was impossible.' And 'Paracelsus,' too, stirred her; but when I recited the thrilling fragment, 'Prospice,' on to that closing rapturous cry--

> 'Then a light, then thy breast,
> O thou soul of my soul! I shall clasp thee again,
> And with God be the rest!'--

the red colour faded from her cheek, her breath came in a sob, and she rose quickly and passed out without a word. Ever after, Browning was among her gods. But when we talked of music, she, adoring Wagner, soared upon the wings of the mighty Tannhauser, far above, into regions unknown, leaving me to walk soberly with Beethoven and Mendelssohn. Yet with all our free, frank talk, there was all the while that in her gentle courtesy which kept me from venturing into any chamber of her life whose door she did not set freely open to me. So I vexed myself about her, and when Mr. Craig returned the next week from the Landing where he had been for some days, my first question was--

'Who is Mrs. Mavor? And how in the name of all that is wonderful and unlikely does she come to be here? And why does she stay?'

He would not answer then; whether it was that his mind was full of the coming struggle, or whether he shrank from the tale, I know not; but that night, when we sat together beside his fire, he told me the story, while I smoked. He was worn with his long, hard drive, and with the burden of his work, but as he went on with his tale, looking into the fire as he told it, he forgot all his present weariness and lived again the scenes he painted for me. This was his story:--

'I remember well my first sight of her, as she sprang from the front seat of the stage to the ground, hardly touching her husband's hand. She looked a mere girl. Let's see--five years ago--she couldn't have been a day over twenty three. She looked barely twenty. Her swift glance swept over the group of miners at the hotel door, and then rested on the mountains standing in all their autumn glory.

'I was proud of our mountains that evening. Turning to her husband, she exclaimed: "O Lewis, are they not grand? and lovely, too?" Every miner lost his heart then and there, but all waited for Abe the driver to give his verdict before venturing an opinion. Abe said nothing until he had taken a preliminary drink, and then, calling all hands to fill up, he lifted his glass high, and said solemnly--

'"Boys, here's to her."

'Like a flash every glass was emptied, and Abe called out, "Fill her up again, boys! My treat!"

'He was evidently quite worked up. Then he began, with solemn emphasis--

'"Boys, you hear me! She's a No. 1, triple X, the pure quill with a bead on it: she's a--," and for the first time in his Black Rock history Abe was stuck for a word. Some one suggested "angel."

'"Angel!" repeated Abe, with infinite contempt. "Angel be blowed," (I paraphrase here); "angels ain't in the same month with her; I'd like to see any blanked angel swing my team around them curves without a shiver."

'"Held the lines herself, Abe?" asked a miner.

'"That's what," said Abe; and then he went off into a fusilade of scientific profanity, expressive of his esteem for the girl who had swung his team round the curves; and the miners nodded to each other, and winked their entire approval of Abe's performance, for this was his specialty.

'Very decent fellow, Abe, but his talk wouldn't print.'

Here Craig paused, as if balancing Abe's virtues and vices.

'Well,' I urged, 'who is she?'

'Oh yes,' he said, recalling himself; 'she is an Edinburgh young lady--met Lewis Mavor, a young Scotch-English man, in London--wealthy, good family, and all that, but fast, and going to pieces at home. His people, who own large shares in these mines here, as a last resort sent him out here to reform. Curiously innocent ideas those old country people have of the reforming properties of this atmosphere! They send their young bloods here to reform. Here! in this devil's camp-ground, where a man's lust is his only law, and when, from sheer monotony, a man must betake himself to the only excitement of the place--that offered by the saloon. Good people in the east hold up holy hands of horror at these godless miners; but I tell you it's asking these boys a good deal to keep straight and clean in a place like this. I take my excitement in fighting the devil and doing my work generally, and that gives me enough; but these poor chaps--hard worked, homeless, with no break or change--God help them and me!' and his voice sank low.

'Well,' I persisted, 'did Mavor reform?'

Again he roused himself. 'Reform? Not exactly. In six-months he had broken through all restraint; and, mind you, not the miners' fault--not a miner helped him down. It was a sight to make angels weep when Mrs. Mavor would come to the saloon door for her husband. Every miner would vanish; they could not look upon her shame, and they would send Mavor forth in the charge of Billy Breen, a queer little chap, who had belonged to the Mavors in some way in the old country, and between them they would get him home. How she stood it puzzles me to this day; but she never made any sign, and her courage never failed. It was always a bright, brave, proud face she held up to the world--except in church; there it was different. I used to preach my sermons, I believe, mostly for her--but never so that she could suspect--as bravely and as cheerily as I could. And as she listened, and especially as she sang--how she used to sing in those days!--there was no touch of pride in her face, though the courage never died out, but appeal, appeal! I could have cursed aloud the cause of her misery, or wept for the pity of it. Before her baby was born he seemed to pull himself together, for he was quite mad about her, and from the day the baby came--talk about miracles!--from that day he never drank a drop. She gave the baby over to him, and the baby simply absorbed him.

'He was a new man. He could not drink whisky and kiss his baby. And the miners--it was really absurd if it were not so pathetic. It was the first baby in Black Rock, and they used to crowd Mavor's shop and peep into the room at the back of it--I forgot to tell you that when he lost his position as manager he opened a hardware shop, for his people chucked him, and he was too proud to write home for money--just for a chance to be asked in to see the baby. I came upon Nixon standing at the back of the shop after he had seen the baby for the first time, sobbing hard, and to my question he replied: "It's just like my own." You can't understand this. But to men who have lived so long in the mountains that they have forgotten what a baby looks like, who have had experience of humanity only in its roughest, foulest form, this little mite, sweet and clean, was like an angel fresh from heaven, the one link in all that black camp that bound them to what was purest and best in their past.

'And to see the mother and her baby handle the miners!

'Oh, it was all beautiful beyond words! I shall never forget the shock I got one night when I found "Old Ricketts" nursing the baby. A drunken old beast he was; but there he was sitting, sober enough, making extraordinary faces at the baby, who was grabbing at his nose and whiskers and cooing in blissful delight. Poor "Old Ricketts" looked as if he had been caught stealing, and muttering something about having to go, gazed wildly round for some place in which to lay the baby, when in came the mother, saying in her own sweet, frank way: "O Mr. Ricketts" (she didn't find out till afterwards his name was Shaw), "would you mind keeping her just a little longer?--I shall be back in a few minutes." And "Old Ricketts" guessed he could wait.

'But in six months mother and baby, between them, transformed "Old Ricketts" into Mr. Shaw, fire-boss of the mines. And then in the evenings, when she would be singing her baby to sleep, the little shop would be full of miners, listening in dead silence to the baby-songs, and the English songs, and the Scotch songs she poured forth without stint, for she sang more for them than for her baby. No wonder they adored her. She was so bright, so gay, she brought light with her when she went into the camp, into the pits--for she went down to see the men work--or into a sick miner's shack; and many a man, lonely and sick for home or wife, or baby or mother, found in that back room cheer and comfort and courage, and to many a poor broken wretch that room became, as one miner put it, "the anteroom to heaven."'

Mr. Craig paused, and I waited. Then he went on slowly--

'For a year and a half that was the happiest home in all the world, till one day--'

He put his face in his hands, and shuddered.

'I don't think I can ever forget the awful horror of that bright fall afternoon, when "Old Ricketts" came breathless to me and gasped, "Come! for the dear Lord's sake," and I rushed after him. At the mouth of the shaft lay three men dead. One was Lewis Mavor. He had gone down to superintend the running of a new drift; the two men, half drunk with Slavin's whisky, set off a shot prematurely, to their own and Mavor's destruction. They were badly burned, but his face was untouched. A miner was sponging off the bloody froth oozing from his lips. The others were standing about waiting for me to speak. But I could find no word, for my heart was sick, thinking, as they were, of the young mother and her baby waiting at home. So I stood, looking stupidly from one to the other, trying to find some reason--coward that I was--why another should bear the news rather than I. And while we stood there, looking at one another in fear, there broke upon us the sound of a voice mounting high above the birch tops, singing--

> "Will ye no' come back again?
> Will ye no' come back again?
> Better lo'ed ye canna be,
> Will ye no' come back again?"

'A strange terror seized us. Instinctively the men closed up in front of the body, and stood in silence. Nearer and nearer came the clear, sweet voice, ringing like a silver bell up the steep--

> "Sweet the lav'rock's note and lang, Liltin' wildly up the glen,
> But aye tae me he sings ae sang,
> Will ye no' come back again?"

'Before the verse was finished "Old Ricketts" had dropped on his knees, sobbing out brokenly, "O God! O God! have pity, have pity, have pity!"--and every man took off his hat. And still the voice came nearer, singing so brightly the refrain,
      '"Will ye no' come back again?'
'It became unbearable. "Old Ricketts" sprang suddenly to his feet, and, gripping me by the arm, said piteously, "Oh, go to her! for Heaven's sake, go to her!" I next remember standing in her path and seeing her holding out her hands full of red lilies, crying out, "Are they not lovely? Lewis is so fond of them!" With the promise of much finer ones I turned her down a path toward the river, talking I know not what folly, till her great eyes grew grave, then anxious, and my tongue stammered and became silent. Then, laying her hand upon my arm, she said with gentle sweetness, "Tell me your trouble, Mr. Craig," and I knew my agony had come, and I burst out, "Oh, if it were only mine!" She turned quite white, and with her deep eyes-- you've noticed her eyes--drawing the truth out of mine, she said, "Is it mine, Mr. Craig, and my baby's?" I waited, thinking with what words to begin. She put one hand to her heart, and with the other caught a little poplar-tree that shivered under her grasp, and said with white lips, but even more gently, "Tell me." I wondered at

my voice being so steady as I said, "Mrs. Mavor, God will help you and your baby. There has been an accident--and it is all over."

'She was a miner's wife, and there was no need for more. I could see the pattern of the sunlight falling through the trees upon the grass. I could hear the murmur of the river, and the cry of the cat-bird in the bushes, but we seemed to be in a strange and unreal world. Suddenly she stretched out her hands to me, and with a little moan said, "Take me to him."

'"Sit down for a moment or two," I entreated.

'"No, no! I am quite ready. See," she added quietly, "I am quite strong."

'I set off by a short cut leading to her home, hoping the men would be there before us; but, passing me, she walked swiftly through the trees, and I followed in fear. As we came near the main path I heard the sound of feet, and I tried to stop her, but she, too, had heard and knew. "Oh, let me go!" she said piteously; "you need not fear." And I had not the heart to stop her. In a little opening among the pines we met the bearers. When the men saw her, they laid their burden gently down upon the carpet of yellow pine-needles, and then, for they had the hearts of true men in them, they went away into the bushes and left her alone with her dead. She went swiftly to his side, making no cry, but kneeling beside him she stroked his face and hands, and touched his curls with her fingers, murmuring all the time soft words of love. "O my darling, my bonnie, bonnie darling, speak to me! Will ye not speak to me just one little word? O my love, my love, my heart's love! Listen, my darling!" And she put her lips to his ear, whispering, and then the awful stillness. Suddenly she lifted her head and scanned his face, and then, glancing round with a wild surprise in her eyes, she cried, "He will not speak to me! Oh, he will not speak to me!" I signed to the men, and as they came forward I went to her and took her hands.

'"Oh," she said with a wail in her voice; "he will not speak to me." The men were sobbing aloud. She looked at them with wide-open eyes of wonder. "Why are they weeping? Will he never speak to me again? Tell me," she insisted gently. The words were running through my head--

'"There's a land that is fairer than day,"

and I said them over to her, holding her hands firmly in mine. She gazed at me as if in a dream, and the light slowly faded from her eyes as she said, tearing her hands from mine and waving them towards the mountains and the woods--

'"But never more here? Never more here?"

'I believe in heaven and the other life, but I confess that for a moment it all seemed shadowy beside the reality of this warm, bright world, full of life and love. She was very ill for two nights, and when the coffin was closed a new baby lay in the father's arms.

'She slowly came back to life, but there were no more songs. The miners still come about her shop, and talk to her baby, and bring her their sorrows and troubles; but though she is always gentle, almost tender, with them, no man ever says "Sing." And that is why I am glad she sang last week; it will be good for her and good for them.'

'Why does she stay?' I asked.

'Mavor's people wanted her to go to them,' he replied.

'They have money--she told me about it, but her heart is in the grave up there under the pines; and besides, she hopes to do something for the miners, and she will not leave them.'

I am afraid I snorted a little impatiently as I said, 'Nonsense! why, with her face, and manner, and voice she could be anything she liked in Edinburgh or in London.'

'And why Edinburgh or London?' he asked coolly.

'Why?' I repeated a little hotly. 'You think this is better?'

'Nazareth was good enough for the Lord of glory,' he answered, with a smile none too bright; but it drew my heart to him, and my heat was gone.

'How long will she stay?' I asked.

'Till her work is done,' he replied.

'And when will that be?' I asked impatiently.

'When God chooses,' he answered gravely; 'and don't you ever think but that it is worth while. One value of work is not that crowds stare at it. Read history, man!'

He rose abruptly and began to walk about. 'And don't miss the whole meaning of the Life that lies at the foundation of your religion. Yes,' he added to himself, 'the work is worth doing--worth even her doing.'

I could not think so then, but the light of the after years proved him wiser than I. A man, to see far, must climb to some height, and I was too much upon the plain in those days to catch even a glimpse of distant sunlit uplands of triumphant achievement that lie beyond the valley of self-sacrifice.

CHAPTER V
THE MAKING OF THE LEAGUE

Thursday morning found Craig anxious, even gloomy, but with fight in every line of his face. I tried to cheer him in my clumsy way by chaffing him about his League. But he did not blaze up as he often did. It was a thing too near his heart for that. He only shrank a little from my stupid chaff and said--

'Don't, old chap; this is a good deal to me. I've tried for two years to get this, and if it falls through now, I shall find it hard to bear.'

Then I repented my light words and said, 'Why! the thing will go sure enough: after that scene in the church they won't go back.'

'Poor fellows!' he said as if to himself; 'whisky is about the only excitement they have, and they find it pretty tough to give it up; and a lot of the men are against the total abstinence idea. It seems rot to them.'

'It is pretty steep,' I said. 'Can't you do without it?'

'No; I fear not. There is nothing else for it. Some of them talk of compromise. They want to quit the saloon and drink quietly in their shacks. The moderate drinker may have his place in other countries, though I can't see it. I haven't thought that out, but here the only safe man is the man who quits it dead and fights it straight; anything else is sheerest humbug and nonsense.'

I had not gone in much for total abstinence up to this time, chiefly because its advocates seemed for the most part to be somewhat ill-balanced; but as I listened to Craig, I began to feel that perhaps there was a total abstinence side to the temperance question; and as to Black Rock, I could see how it must be one thing or the other.

We found Mrs. Mavor brave and bright. She shared Mr. Craig's anxiety but not his gloom. Her courage was of that serene kind that refuses to believe defeat possible, and lifts the spirit into the triumph of final victory. Through the past week she had been carefully disposing her forces and winning recruits. And yet she never seemed to urge or persuade the men; but as evening after evening the miners dropped into the cosy room downstairs, with her talk and her songs she charmed them till they were wholly hers. She took for granted their loyalty, trusted them utterly, and so made it difficult for them to be other than true men.

That night Mrs. Mavor's large storeroom, which had been fitted up with seats, was crowded with miners when Mr. Craig and I entered.

After a glance over the crowd, Craig said, 'There's the manager; that means war.' And I saw a tall man, very fair, whose chin fell away to the vanishing point, and whose hair was parted in the middle, talking to Mrs. Mavor. She was dressed in some rich soft stuff that became her well. She was looking beautiful as ever, but there was something quite new in her manner. Her air of good-fellowship was gone, and she was the high-bred lady, whose gentle dignity and sweet grace, while very winning, made familiarity impossible.

The manager was doing his best, and appeared to be well pleased with himself. 'She'll get him if any one can. I failed,' said Craig.

I stood looking at the men, and a fine lot of fellows they were. Free, easy, bold in their bearing, they gave no sign of rudeness; and, from their frequent glances toward Mrs. Mavor, I could see they were always conscious of her presence. No men are so truly gentle as are the Westerners in the presence of a good woman. They were evidently of all classes and ranks originally, but now, and in this country of real measurements, they ranked simply according to the 'man' in them. 'See that handsome, young chap of dissipated appearance?' said Craig; 'that's Vernon Winton, an Oxford graduate, blue blood, awfully plucky, but quite gone. When he gets repentant, instead of shooting himself, he comes to Mrs. Mavor. Fact.'

'From Oxford University to Black Rock mining camp is something of a step,' I replied.

'That queer-looking little chap in the corner is Billy Breen. How in the world has he got here?' went on Mr. Craig. Queer-looking he was. A little man, with a small head set on heavy square shoulders, long arms, and huge hands that sprawled all over his body; altogether a most ungainly specimen of humanity.

By this time Mrs. Mavor had finished with the manager, and was in the centre of a group of miners. Her grand air was all gone, and she was their comrade, their friend, one of themselves. Nor did she assume the role of entertainer, but rather did she, with half-shy air, cast herself upon their chivalry, and they were too truly gentlemen to fail her. It is hard to make Western men, and especially old-timers, talk. But this gift was hers, and it stirred my admiration to see her draw on a grizzled veteran to tell how, twenty years ago, he had crossed the Great Divide, and had seen and done what no longer fell to men to see or do in these new days. And so she won the old-timer. But it was beautiful to see the innocent guile with which she caught Billy Breen, and drew him to her corner near the organ. What she was saying I knew not, but poor Billy was protesting, waving his big hands.

The meeting came to order, with Shaw in the chair, and the handsome young Oxford man secretary. Shaw stated the object of the meeting in a few halting words; but when he came to speak of the pleasure he and all felt in being together in that room, his words flowed in a stream, warm and full. Then there was a pause, and Mr. Craig was called. But he knew better than to speak at that point. Finally Nixon rose hesitatingly; but, as he caught a bright smile from Mrs. Mavor, he straightened himself as if for a fight.

'I ain't no good at makin' speeches,' he began; 'but it ain't speeches we want. We've got somethin' to do, and what we want to know is how to do it. And to be right plain, we want to know how to drive this cursed whisky out of Black Rock. You all know what it's doing for us--at least for some of us. And it's time to stop it now, or for some of us it'll mighty soon be too late. And the only way to stop its work is to quit drinkin' it and help others to quit. I hear some talk of a League, and what I say is, if it's a League out and out against whisky, a Total Abstinence right to the ground, then I'm with it--that's my talk--I move we make that kind of League.'

Nixon sat down amid cheers and a chorus of remarks, 'Good man!' 'That's the talk!' 'Stay with it!' but he waited for the smile and the glance that came to him from the beautiful face in the corner, and with that he seemed content.

Again there was silence. Then the secretary rose with a slight flush upon his handsome, delicate face, and seconded the motion. If they would pardon a personal reference he would give them his reasons. He had come to this country to make his fortune; now he was anxious to make enough to enable him to go home with some degree of honour. His home held everything that was dear to him. Between him and that home, between him and all that was good and beautiful and honourable, stood whisky. 'I am ashamed to confess,' and the flush deepened on his cheek, and his lips grew thinner, 'that I feel the need of some such league.' His handsome face, his perfect style of address, learned possibly in the 'Union,' but, more than all, his show of nerve--for these men knew how to value that--made a strong impression on his audience; but there were no following cheers.

Mr. Craig appeared hopeful; but on Mrs. Mavor's face there was a look of wistful, tender pity, for she knew how much the words had cost the lad.

Then up rose a sturdy, hard-featured man, with a burr in his voice that proclaimed his birth. His name was George Crawford, I afterwards learned, but every one called him Geordie. He was a character in his way, fond of his glass; but though he was never known to refuse a drink, he was never known to be drunk. He took his drink, for the most part, with bread and cheese in his own shack, or with a friend or two in a sober, respectable way, but never could be induced to join the wild carousals in Slavin's saloon. He made the highest wages, but was far too true a Scot to spend his money recklessly. Every one waited eagerly to hear Geordie's mind. He spoke solemnly, as befitted a Scotsman expressing a deliberate opinion, and carefully, as if choosing his best English, for when Geordie became excited no one in Black Rock could understand him.

'Maister Chairman,' said Geordie, 'I'm aye for temperance in a' things.' There was a shout of laughter, at which Geordie gazed round in pained surprise. 'I'll no' deny,' he went on in an explanatory tone, 'that I tak ma mornin', an' maybe a nip at noon; an' a wee drap aifter wark in the evenin', an' whiles a sip o' toddy wi' a freen thae cauld nichts. But I'm no' a guzzler, an' I dinna gang in wi' thae loons flingin' aboot guid money.'

'And that's thrue for you, me bye,' interrupted a rich Irish brogue, to the delight of the crowd and the amazement of Geordie, who went calmly on--

'An' I canna bide yon saloon whaur they sell sic awfu'-like stuff--it's mair like lye nor guid whisky,--and whaur ye're never sure o' yer richt change. It's an awfu'-like place; man!'--and Geordie began to warm up--'ye can juist smell the sulphur when ye gang in. But I dinna care aboot thae Temperance Soceeities, wi' their pledges an' havers; an' I canna see what hairm can come till a man by takin' a bottle o' guid Glenlivet hame wi' him. I canna bide thae teetotal buddies.'

Geordie's speech was followed by loud applause, partly appreciative of Geordie himself, but largely sympathetic with his position.

Two or three men followed in the same strain advocating a league for mutual improvement and social purposes, but without the teetotal pledge; they were against the saloon, but didn't see why they should not take a drink now and then.

Finally the manager rose to support his 'friend, Mistah--ah--Cwafoad,' ridiculing the idea of a total abstinence pledge as fanatical and indeed 'absuad.' He was opposed to the saloon, and would like to see a club formed, with a comfortable club-room, books, magazines, pictures, games, anything, 'dontcheknow, to make the time pass pleasantly'; but it was 'absuad to ask men to abstain fwom a pwopah use of--aw--nouwishing dwinks,' because some men made beasts of themselves. He concluded by offering $50.00 towards the support of such a club.

The current of feeling was setting strongly against the total abstinence idea, and Craig's face was hard and his eyes gleamed like coals. Then he did a bit of generalship. He proposed that since they had the two plans clearly before them they should take a few minutes' intermission in which to make up their minds, and he was sure they would be glad to have Mrs. Mavor sing. In the interval the men talked in groups, eagerly, even fiercely, hampered seriously in the forceful expression of their opinion by the presence of Mrs. Mavor, who glided from group to group, dropping a word here and a smile there. She reminded me of a general riding along the ranks, bracing his men for the coming battle. She paused beside Geordie, spoke earnestly for a few moments, while Geordie gazed solemnly at her, and then she came back to Billy in the corner near me. What she was saying I could not hear, but poor Billy was protesting, spreading his hands out aimlessly before him, but gazing at her the while in dumb admiration. Then she came to me. 'Poor Billy, he was good to my husband,' she said softly, 'and he has a good heart.'

'He's not much to look at,' I could not help saying.

'The oyster hides its pearl,' she answered, a little reproachfully.

'The shell is apparent enough,' I replied, for the mischief was in me.

'Ah yes,' she replied softly, 'but it is the pearl we love.'

I moved over beside Billy, whose eyes were following Mrs. Mavor as she went to speak to Mr. Craig. 'Well,' I said; 'you all seem to have a high opinion of her.'

'An 'igh hopinion,' he replied, in deep scorn. 'An 'igh hopinion, you calls it.'

'What would you call it?' I asked, wishing to draw him out.

'Oi don't call it nothink,' he replied, spreading out his rough hands.

'She seems very nice,' I said indifferently.

He drew his eyes away from Mrs. Mavor, and gave attention to me for the first time.

'Nice!' he repeated with fine contempt; and then he added impressively, 'Them as don't know shouldn't say nothink.'

'You are right,' I answered earnestly, 'and I am quite of your opinion.'

He gave me a quick glance out of his little, deep-set, dark-blue eyes, and opened his heart to me. He told me, in his quaint speech, how again and again she had taken him in and nursed him, and encouraged him, and sent him out with a new heart for his battle, until, for very shame's sake at his own miserable weakness, he had kept out of her way for many months, going steadily down.

'Now, oi hain't got no grip; but when she says to me to-night, says she, "Oh, Billy"--she calls me Billy to myself' (this with a touch of pride)--'"oh, Billy," says she, "we must 'ave a total habstinence league to-night, and oi want you to 'elp!" and she keeps a-lookin' at me with those heyes o' hern till, if you believe me, sir,' lowering his voice to an emphatic whisper, 'though oi knowed oi couldn't 'elp none, afore oi knowed oi promised 'er oi would. It's 'er heyes. When them heyes says "do," hup you steps and "does."'

I remembered my first look into her eyes, and I could quite understand Billy's submission. Just as she began to sing I went over to Geordie and took my seat beside him. She began with an English slumber song, 'Sleep, Baby, Sleep'--one of Barry Cornwall's, I think,--and then sang a love-song with the refrain, 'Love once again'; but no thrills came to me, and I began to wonder if her spell over me was broken. Geordie, who had been listening somewhat indifferently, encouraged me, however, by saying, 'She's just pittin' aff time with thae feckless sangs; man, there's nae grup till them.' But when, after a few minutes' pause, she began 'My Ain Fireside,' Geordie gave a sigh of satisfaction. 'Ay, that's somethin' like,' and when she finished the first verse he gave me a dig in the ribs with his elbow that took my breath away, saying in a whisper, 'Man, hear till yon, wull ye?' And again I found the spell upon me. It was not the voice after all, but the great soul behind that thrilled and compelled. She was seeing, feeling, living what she sang, and her voice showed us her heart. The cosy fireside, with its bonnie, blithe blink, where no care could abide, but only peace and love, was vividly present to her, and as she sang we saw it too. When she came to the last verse--

> 'When I draw in my stool
> On my cosy hearth-stane,
> My heart loups sae licht
> I scarce ken't for my ain,'

there was a feeling of tears in the flowing song, and we knew the words had brought her a picture of the fireside that would always seem empty. I felt the tears in my eyes, and, wondering at myself, I cast a stealthy glance at the men about me; and I saw that they, too, were looking through their hearts' windows upon firesides and ingle-neuks that gleamed from far.

And then she sang 'The Auld Hoose,' and Geordie, giving me another poke, said, 'That's ma ain sang,' and when I asked him what he meant, he whispered fiercely, 'Wheesht, man!' and I did, for his face looked dangerous.

In a pause between the verses I heard Geordie saying to himself, 'Ay, I maun gie it up, I doot.'

'What?' I ventured.

'Naething ava.' And then he added impatiently, 'Man, but ye're an inqueesitive buddie,' after which I subsided into silence.

Immediately upon the meeting being called to order, Mr. Craig made his speech, and it was a fine bit of work. Beginning with a clear statement of the object in view, he set in contrast the two kinds of leagues proposed. One, a league of men who would take whisky in moderation; the other, a league of men who were pledged to drink none themselves, and to prevent in every honourable way others from drinking. There was no long argument, but he spoke at white heat; and as he appealed to the men to think, each not of himself alone, but of the others as well, the yearning, born of his long months of desire and of toil, vibrated in his voice and reached to the heart. Many men looked uncomfortable and uncertain, and even the manager looked none too cheerful.

At this critical moment the crowd got a shock. Billy Breen shuffled out to the front, and, in a voice shaking with nervousness and emotion, began to speak, his large, coarse hands wandering tremulously about.

'Oi hain't no bloomin' temperance horator, and mayhap oi hain't no right to speak 'ere, but oi got somethin' to saigh (say) and oi'm agoin' to saigh it.

'Parson, 'ee says is it wisky or no wisky in this 'ere club? If ye hask me, wich (which) ye don't, then no wisky, says oi; and if ye hask why?--look at me! Once oi could mine more coal than hany man in the camp; now oi hain't fit to be a sorter. Once oi 'ad some pride and hambition; now oi 'angs round awaitin' for some one to saigh, "Ere, Billy, 'ave summat." Once oi made good paigh (pay), and sent it 'ome regular to my poor old mother (she's in the wukus now, she is); oi hain't sent 'er hany for a year and a 'alf. Once Billy was a good fellow and 'ad plenty o' friends; now Slavin 'isself kicks un hout, 'ee does. Why? why?' His voice rose to a shriek. 'Because when Billy 'ad money in 'is pocket, hevery man in this bloomin' camp as meets un at hevery corner says, "'Ello, Billy, wat'll ye 'ave?" And there's wisky at Slavin's, and there's wisky in the shacks, and hevery 'oliday and hevery Sunday there's wisky, and w'en ye feel bad it's wisky, and w'en ye feel good it's wisky, and heverywhere and halways it's wisky, wisky, wisky! And now ye're goin' to stop it, and 'ow? T' manager, 'ee says picters and magazines. 'Ee takes 'is wine and 'is beer like a gentleman, 'ee does, and 'ee don't 'ave no use for Billy Breen. Billy, 'ee's a beast, and t' manager, 'ee kicks un hout. But supposin' Billy wants to stop bein' a beast, and starts a-tryin' to be a man again, and w'en 'ee gets good an' dry, along comes some un and says, "'Ello, Billy, 'ave a smile," it hain't picters nor magazines 'ud stop un then. Picters and magazines! Gawd 'elp the man as hain't nothin' but picters and magazines to 'elp un w'en 'ee's got a devil hinside and a devil houtside a-shovin' and a-drawin' of un down to 'ell. And that's w'ere oi'm a-goin' straight, and yer bloomin' League, wisky or no wisky, can't help me. But,' and he lifted his trembling hands above his head, 'if ye stop the wisky a-flowin' round this camp, ye'll stop some of these lads that's a-followin' me 'ard. Yes, you! and you! and you!' and his voice rose to a wild scream as he shook a trembling finger at one and another.

'Man, it's fair gruesome tae hear him,' said Geordie; 'he's no' canny'; and reaching out for Billy as he went stumbling past, he pulled him down to a seat beside him, saying, 'Sit doon, lad, sit doon. We'll mak a man o' ye yet.' Then he rose and, using many r's, said, 'Maister Chairman, a' doot we'll juist hae to gie it up.'

'Give it up?' called out Nixon. 'Give up the League?'

'Na! na! lad, but juist the wee drap whusky. It's nae that guid onyway, and it's a terrible price. Man, gin ye gang tae Henderson's in Buchanan Street, in Gleska, ye ken, ye'll get mair for three-an'-saxpence than ye wull at Slavin's for five dollars. An' it'll no' pit ye mad like yon stuff, but it gangs doon smooth an' saft-like. But' (regretfully) 'ye'll no' can get it here; an' a'm thinkin' a'll juist sign yon teetotal thing.' And up he strode to the table and put his name down in the book Craig had ready. Then to Billy he said, 'Come' awa, lad! pit yer name doon, an' we'll stan' by ye.'

Poor Billy looked around helplessly, his nerve all gone, and sat still. There was a swift rustle of garments, and Mrs. Mavor was beside him, and, in a voice that only Billy and I could hear, said, 'You'll sign with, me, Billy?'

Billy gazed at her with a hopeless look in his eyes, and shook his little, head. She leaned slightly toward him, smiling brightly, and, touching his arm gently, said--

'Come, Billy, there's no fear,' and in a lower voice, 'God will help you.'

As Billy went up, following Mrs. Mavor close, a hush fell on the men until he had put his name to the pledge; then they came up, man by man, and signed. But Craig sat with his head down till I touched his shoulder. He took my hand and held it fast, saying over and over, under his breath, 'Thank God, thank God!'

And so the League was made.

CHAPTER VI
BLACK ROCK RELIGION

When I grow weary with the conventions of religion, and sick in my soul from feeding upon husks, that the churches too often offer me, in the shape of elaborate service and eloquent discourses, so that in my sickness I doubt and doubt, then I go back to the communion in Black Rock and the days preceding it, and the fever and the weariness leave me, and I grow humble and strong. The simplicity and rugged grandeur of the faith, the humble gratitude of the rough men I see about the table, and the calm radiance of one saintly face, rest and recall me.

Not its most enthusiastic apologist would call Black Rock a religious community, but it possessed in a marked degree that eminent Christian virtue of tolerance. All creeds, all shades of religious opinion, were allowed, and it was generally conceded that one was as good as another. It is fair to say, however, that Black Rock's catholicity was negative rather than positive. The only religion objectionable was that insisted upon as a necessity. It never occurred to any one to consider religion other than as a respectable, if not ornamental, addition to life in older lands.

During the weeks following the making of the League, however, this negative attitude towards things religious gave place to one of keen investigation and criticism. The indifference passed away, and with it, in a large measure, the tolerance. Mr. Craig was responsible for the former of these changes, but hardly, in fairness, could he be held responsible for the latter. If any one, more than another, was to be blamed for the rise of intolerance in the village, that man was Geordie Crawford. He had his 'lines' from the Established Kirk of Scotland, and when Mr. Craig announced his intention of having the Sacrament of the Lord's Supper observed, Geordie produced his 'lines' and promptly handed them in. As no other man in the village was equipped with like spiritual credentials, Geordie constituted himself a kind of kirk-session, charged with the double duty of guarding the entrance to the Lord's Table, and of keeping an eye upon the theological opinions of the community, and more particularly upon such members of it as gave evidence of possessing any opinions definite enough for statement.

It came to be Mr. Craig's habit to drop into the League-room, and toward the close of the evening to have a short Scripture lesson from the Gospels. Geordie's opportunity came after the meeting was over and Mr. Craig had gone away. The men would hang about and talk the lesson over, expressing opinions favourable or unfavourable as appeared to them good. Then it was that all sorts of views, religious and otherwise, were aired and examined. The originality of the ideas, the absolute disregard of the authority of church or creed, the frankness with which opinions were stated, and the forcefulness of the language in which they were expressed, combined to make the discussions altogether marvellous. The passage between Abe Baker, the stage-driver, and Geordie was particularly rich. It followed upon a very telling lesson on the parable of the Pharisee and the Publican.

The chief actors in that wonderful story were transferred to the Black Rock stage, and were presented in miner's costume. Abe was particularly well pleased with the scoring of the 'blanked old rooster who crowed so blanked high,' and somewhat incensed at the quiet remark interjected by Geordie, 'that it was nae credit till a man tae be a sinner'; and when Geordie went on to urge the importance of right conduct and respectability, Abe was led to pour forth vials of contemptuous wrath upon the Pharisees and hypocrites who thought themselves better than other people. But Geordie was quite unruffled, and lamented the ignorance of men who, brought up in 'Epeescopawlyun or Methody' churches, could hardly be expected to detect the Antinomian or Arminian heresies.

'Aunty Nomyun or Uncle Nomyun,' replied Abe, boiling hot, 'my mother was a Methodist, and I'll back any blanked Methodist against any blankety blank long-faced, lantern-jawed, skinflint Presbyterian,' and this he was eager to maintain to any man's satisfaction if he would step outside.

Geordie was quite unmoved, but hastened to assure Abe that he meant no dis-respect to his mother, who he had 'nae doot was a clever enough buddie, tae judge by her son.' Abe was speedily appeased, and offered to set up the drinks all round. But Geordie, with evident reluctance, had to decline, saying, 'Na, na, lad, I'm a League man ye ken,' and I was sure that Geordie at that moment felt that member-ship in the League had its drawbacks.

Nor was Geordie too sure of Craig's orthodoxy; while as to Mrs. Mavor, whose slave he was, he was in the habit of lamenting her doctrinal condition--

'She's a fine wumman, nae doot; but, puir cratur, she's fair carried awa wi' the errors o' thae Epeescopawlyuns.'

It fell to Geordie, therefore, as a sacred duty, in view of the laxity of those who seemed to be the pillars of the Church, to be all the more watchful and unyielding. But he was delightfully inconsistent when confronted with particulars. In conver-sation with him one night after one of the meetings, when he had been specially hard upon the ignorant and godless, I innocently changed the subject to Billy Breen, whom Geordie had taken to his shack since the night of the League. He was very proud of Billy's success in the fight against whisky, the credit of which he divided unevenly between Mrs. Mavor and himself.

'He's fair daft aboot her,' he explained to me, 'an' I'll no' deny but she's a great help, ay, a verra conseederable asseestance; but, man, she doesna ken the whusky, an' the inside o' a man that's wantin' it. Ay, puir buddie, she diz her pairt, an' when ye're a bit restless an thrawn aifter yer day's wark, it's like a walk in a bonnie glen on a simmer eve, with the birds liltin' aboot, tae sit in yon roomie and hear her sing; but when the night is on, an' ye canna sleep, but wauken wi' an' awfu' thurst and wi' dreams o' cosy firesides, and the bonnie sparklin' glosses, as it is wi' puir Billy, ay, it's then ye need a man wi' a guid grup beside ye.'

'What do you do then, Geordie?' I asked.

'Oo ay, I juist gang for a bit walk wi' the lad, and then pits the kettle on an' maks a cup o' tea or coffee, an' aff he gangs tae sleep like a bairn.'

'Poor Billy,' I said pityingly, 'there's no hope for him in the future, I fear.'

'Hoot awa, man,' said Geordie quickly. 'Ye wadna keep oot a puir cratur frae creepin' in, that's daein' his best?'

'But, Geordie,' I remonstrated, 'he doesn't know anything of the doctrines. I don't believe he could give us "The Chief End of Man."'

'An' wha's tae blame for that?' said Geordie, with fine indignation. 'An' maybe you remember the prood Pharisee and the puir wumman that cam' creepin' in ahint the Maister.'

The mingled tenderness and indignation in Geordie's face were beautiful to see, so I meekly answered, 'Well, I hope Mr. Craig won't be too strict with the boys.'

Geordie shot a suspicious glance at me, but I kept my face like a summer morn, and he replied cautiously--

'Ay, he's no' that streect: but he maun exerceese discreemination.'

Geordie was none the less determined, however, that Billy should 'come forrit'; but as to the manager, who was a member of the English Church, and some others who had been confirmed years ago, and had forgotten much and denied more, he was extremely doubtful, and expressed himself in very decided words to the minister--

'Ye'll no' be askin' forrit thae Epeescopawlyun buddies. They juist ken naething ava.'

But Mr. Craig looked at him for a moment and said, "Him that cometh unto Me I will in no wise cast out,"' and Geordie was silent, though he continued doubtful.

With all these somewhat fantastic features, however, there was no mistaking the earnest spirit of the men. The meetings grew larger every night, and the interest became more intense. The singing became different. The men no longer simply shouted, but as Mr. Craig would call attention to the sentiment of the hymn, the voices would attune themselves to the words. Instead of encouraging anything like emotional excitement, Mr. Craig seemed to fear it.

'These chaps are easily stirred up,' he would say, 'and I am anxious that they should know exactly what they are doing. It is far too serious a business to trifle with.'

Although Graeme did not go downstairs to the meetings, he could not but feel the throb of the emotion beating in the heart of the community. I used to detail for his benefit, and sometimes for his amusement, the incidents of each night. But I never felt quite easy in dwelling upon the humorous features in Mrs. Mavor's presence, although Craig did not appear to mind. His manner with Graeme was perfect. Openly anxious to win him to his side, he did not improve the occasion and vex him with exhortation. He would not take him at a disadvantage, though, as I afterwards found, this was not his sole reason for his method. Mrs. Mavor, too, showed herself in wise and tender light. She might have been his sister, so frank was she and so openly affectionate, laughing at his fretfulness and soothing his weariness.

Never were better comrades than we four, and the bright days speeding so swiftly on drew us nearer to one another.

But the bright days came to an end; for Graeme, when once he was able to go about, became anxious to get back to the camp. And so the last day came, a day I remember well. It was a bright, crisp winter day.

The air was shimmering in the frosty light. The mountains, with their shining heads piercing through light clouds into that wonderful blue of the western sky, and their feet pushed into the pine masses, gazed down upon Black Rock with calm, kindly looks on their old grey faces. How one grows to love them, steadfast old friends! Far up among the pines we could see the smoke of the engine at the works, and so still and so clear was the mountain air that we could hear the puff of the steam, and from far down the river the murmur of the rapids. The majestic silence, the tender beauty, the peace, the loneliness, too, came stealing in upon us, as we three, leaving Mrs. Mavor behind us, marched arm-in-arm down the street. We had not gone far on our way, when Graeme, turning round, stood a moment looking back, then waved his hand in farewell. Mrs. Mavor was at her window, smiling and waving in return. They had grown to be great friends these two; and seemed to have arrived at some understanding. Certainly, Graeme's manner to her was not that he bore to other women. His half-quizzical, somewhat superior air of mocking devotion gave place to a simple, earnest, almost tender, respect, very new to him, but very winning.

As he stood there waving his farewell, I glanced at his face and saw for a moment what I had not seen for years, a faint flush on Graeme's cheek and a light of simple, earnest faith in his eyes. It reminded me of my first look of him when he had come up for his matriculation to the 'Varsity. He stood on the campus looking up at the noble old pile, and there was the same bright, trustful, earnest look on his boyish face.

I know not what spirit possessed me; it may have been the pain of the memory working in me, but I said, coarsely enough, 'It's no use, Graeme, my boy; I would fall in love with her myself, but there would be no chance even for me.'

The flush slowly darkened as he turned and said deliberately--

'It's not like you, Connor, to be an ass of that peculiar kind. Love!--not exactly! She won't fall in love unless--' and he stopped abruptly with his eyes upon Craig.

But Craig met him with unshrinking gaze, quietly remarking, 'Her heart is under the pines'; and we moved on, each thinking his own thoughts, and guessing at the thoughts of the others.

We were on our way to Craig's shack, and as we passed the saloon Slavin stepped from the door with a salutation. Graeme paused. 'Hello, Slavin! I got rather the worst of it, didn't I?'

Slavin came near, and said earnestly, 'It was a dirty thrick altogether; you'll not think it was moine, Mr. Graeme.'

'No, no, Slavin! you stood up like a man,' said Graeme cheerfully.

'And you bate me fair; an' bedad it was a nate one that laid me out; an' there's no grudge in me heart till ye.'

'All right, Slavin; we'll perhaps understand each other better after this.'

'An' that's thrue for yez, sor; an' I'll see that your byes don't get any more than they ask for,' replied Slavin, backing away.

'And I hope that won't be much,' put in Mr. Craig; but Slavin only grinned.

When we came to Craig's shack Graeme was glad to rest in the big chair.

Craig made him a cup of tea, while I smoked, admiring much the deft neatness of the minister's housekeeping, and the gentle, almost motherly, way he had with Graeme.

In our talk we drifted into the future, and Craig let us see what were his ambitions. The railway was soon to come; the resources were, as yet, unexplored, but enough was known to assure a great future for British Columbia. As he talked his enthusiasm grew, and carried us away. With the eye of a general he surveyed the country, fixed the strategic points which the Church must seize upon. Eight good men would hold the country from Fort Steele to the coast, and from Kootenay to Cariboo.

'The Church must be in with the railway; she must have a hand in the shaping of the country. If society crystallises without her influence, the country is lost, and British Columbia will be another trap-door to the bottomless pit.'

'What do you propose?' I asked.

'Organising a little congregation here in Black Rock.'

'How many will you get?'

'Don't know.'

'Pretty hopeless business,' I said.

'Hopeless! hopeless!' he cried; 'there were only twelve of us at first to follow Him, and rather a poor lot they were. But He braced them up, and they conquered the world.'

'But surely things are different,' said Graeme.

'Things? Yes! yes! But He is the same.' His face had an exalted look, and his eyes were gazing into far-away places.

'A dozen men in Black Rock with some real grip of Him would make things go. We'll get them, too,' he went on in growing excitement. 'I believe in my soul we'll get them.'

'Look here, Craig; if you organise I'd like to join,' said Graeme impulsively. 'I don't believe much in your creed or your Church, but I'll be blowed if I don't believe in you.'

Craig looked at him with wistful eyes, and shook his head. 'It won't do, old chap, you know. I can't hold you. You've got to have a grip of some one better than I am; and then, besides, I hardly like asking you now'; he hesitated--'well, to be out-and-out, this step must be taken not for my sake, nor for any man's sake, and I fancy that perhaps you feel like pleasing me just now a little.'

'That I do, old fellow,' said Graeme, putting out his hand. 'I'll be hanged if I won't do anything you say.'

'That's why I won't say,' replied Craig. Then reverently he added, 'the organisation is not mine. It is my Master's.'

'When are you going to begin?' asked Graeme.

'We shall have our communion service in two weeks, and that will be our roll-call.'

'How many will answer?' I asked doubtfully.

'I know of three,' he said quietly.

'Three! There are two hundred miners and one hundred and fifty lumbermen! Three!' and Graeme looked at him in amazement. 'You think it worth while to organise three?'

'Well,' replied Craig, smiling for the first time, 'the organisation won't be elaborate, but it will be effective, and, besides, loyalty demands obedience.'

We sat long that afternoon talking, shrinking from the breaking up; for we knew that we were about to turn down a chapter in our lives which we should delight to linger over in after days. And in my life there is but one brighter. At last we said good-bye and drove away; and though many farewells have come in between that day and this, none is so vividly present to me as that between us three men. Craig's manner with me was solemn enough. '"He that loveth his life"; good-bye, don't fool with this,' was what he said to me. But when he turned to Graeme his whole face lit up. He took him by the shoulders and gave him a little shake, looking into his eyes, and saying over and over in a low, sweet tone--

'You'll come, old chap, you'll come, you'll come. Tell me you'll come.'

And Graeme could say nothing in reply, but only looked at him. Then they silently shook hands, and we drove off. But long after we had got over the mountain and into the winding forest road on the way to the lumber-camp the voice kept vibrating in my heart, 'You'll come, you'll come,' and there was a hot pain in my throat.

We said little during the drive to the camp. Graeme was thinking hard, and made no answer when I spoke to him two or three times, till we came to the deep shadows of the pine forest, when with a little shiver he said--

'It is all a tangle--a hopeless tangle.'

'Meaning what?' I asked.

'This business of religion--what quaint varieties--Nelson's, Geordie's, Billy Breen's--if he has any--then Mrs. Mavor's--she is a saint, of course--and that fellow Craig's. What a trump he is!--and without his religion he'd be pretty much like the rest of us. It is too much for me.'

His mystery was not mine. The Black Rock varieties of religion were certainly startling; but there was undoubtedly the streak of reality though them all, and that discovery I felt to be a distinct gain.

CHAPTER VII
THE FIRST BLACK ROCK COMMUNION

The gleam of the great fire through the windows of the great camp gave a kindly welcome as we drove into the clearing in which the shanties stood. Graeme was greatly touched at his enthusiastic welcome by the men. At the supper-table he made a little speech of thanks for their faithfulness during his absence, specially commending the care and efficiency of Mr. Nelson, who had had charge of the camp. The men cheered wildly, Baptiste's shrill voice leading all. Nelson being called upon, expressed in a few words his pleasure at seeing the Boss back, and thanked the men for their support while he had been in charge.

The men were for making a night of it; but fearing the effect upon Graeme, I spoke to Nelson, who passed the word, and in a short time the camp was quiet. As we sauntered from the grub-camp to the office where was our bed, we paused to take in the beauty of the night. The moon rode high over the peaks of the mountains, flooding the narrow valley with mellow light. Under her magic the rugged peaks softened their harsh lines and seemed to lean lovingly toward us. The dark pine masses stood silent as in breathless adoration; the dazzling snow lay like a garment over all the open spaces in soft, waving folds, and crowned every stump with a quaintly shaped nightcap. Above the camps the smoke curled up from the camp-fires, standing like pillars of cloud that kept watch while men slept. And high over all the deep blue night sky, with its star jewels, sprang like the roof of a great cathedral from range to range, covering us in its kindly shelter. How homelike and safe seemed the valley with its mountain-sides, its sentinel trees and arching roof of jewelled sky! Even the night seemed kindly, and friendly the stars; and the lone cry of the wolf from the deep forest seemed like the voice of a comrade.

'How beautiful! too beautiful!' said Graeme, stretching out his arms. 'A night like this takes the heart out of me.'

I stood silent, drinking in at every sense the night with its wealth of loveliness.

'What is it I want?' he went on. 'Why does the night make my heart ache? There are things to see and things to hear just beyond me; I cannot get to them.' The gay, careless look was gone from his face, his dark eyes were wistful with yearning.

'I often wonder if life has nothing better for me,' he continued with his heart-ache voice.

I said no word, but put my arm within his. A light appeared in the stable. Glad of a diversion, I said, 'What is the light? Let us go and see.'

'Sandy, taking a last look at his team, like enough.'

We walked slowly toward the stable, speaking no word. As we neared the door we heard the sound of a voice in the monotone of one reading. I stepped forward and looked through a chink between the logs. Graeme was about to open the door, but I held up my hand and beckoned him to me. In a vacant stall, where was a pile of straw, a number of men were grouped. Sandy, leaning against the tying-post upon which the stable-lantern hung, was reading; Nelson was kneeling in front of him and gazing into the gloom beyond; Baptiste lay upon his stomach, his chin in his hands and his upturned eyes fastened upon Sandy's face; Lachlan Campbell sat with his hands clasped about his knees, and two other men sat near him. Sandy was reading the undying story of the Prodigal, Nelson now and then stopping him to make a remark. It was a scene I have never been able to forget. To-day I pause in my tale, and see it as clearly as when I looked through the chink upon it years ago. The long, low stable, with log walls and upright hitching-poles; the dim outlines of the horses in the gloom of the background, and the little group of rough, almost savage-looking men, with faces wondering and reverent, lit by the misty light of the stable-lantern.

After the reading, Sandy handed the book to Nelson, who put it in his pocket, saying, 'That's for us, boys, ain't it?'

'Ay,' said Lachlan; 'it is often that has been read in my hearing, but I am afraid it will not be for me whatever,' and he swayed himself slightly as he spoke, and his voice was full of pain.

'The minister said I might come,' said old Nelson, earnestly and hopefully.

'Ay, but you are not Lachlan Campbell, and you hef not had his privileges. My father was a godly elder in the Free Church of Scotland, and never a night or morning but we took the Books.'

'Yes, but He said "any man,"' persisted Nelson, putting his hand on Lachlan's knee. But Lachlan shook his head.

'Dat young feller,' said Baptiste; 'wha's hees nem, heh?'

'He has no name. It is just a parable,' explained Sandy.

'He's got no nem? He's just a parom'ble? Das no young feller?' asked Baptiste anxiously; 'das mean noting?'

Then Nelson took him in hand and explained to him the meaning, while Baptiste listened even more eagerly, ejaculating softly, 'ah, voila! bon! by gar!' When Nelson had finished he broke out, 'Dat young feller, his name Baptiste, heh? and de old Fadder he's le bon Dieu? Bon! das good story for me. How you go back? You go to de pries'?'

'The book doesn't say priest or any one else,' said Nelson. 'You go back in yourself, you see?'

'Non; das so, sure nuff. Ah!'--as if a light broke in upon him--'you go in your own self. You make one leetle prayer. You say, "Le bon Fadder, oh! I want come back, I so tire, so hongree, so sorree"? He, say, "Come right 'long." Ah! das fuss-rate. Nelson, you make one leetle prayer for Sandy and me.'

And Nelson lifted up his face and said: 'Father, we're all gone far away; we have spent all, we are poor, we are tired of it all; we want to feel different, to be different; we want to come back. Jesus came to save us from our sins; and he said if we came He wouldn't cast us out, no matter how bad we were, if we only came to Him. Oh, Jesus Christ'--and his old, iron face began to work, and two big tears slowly came from under his eyelids--'we are a poor lot, and I'm the worst of the lot, and we are trying to find the way. Show us how to get back. Amen.'

'Bon!' said Baptiste. 'Das fetch Him sure!'

Graeme pulled me away, and without a word we went into the office and drew up to the little stove. Graeme was greatly moved.

'Did you ever see anything like that?' he asked. 'Old Nelson! the hardest, savagest, toughest old sinner in the camp, on his knees before a lot of men!'

'Before God,' I could not help saying, for the thing seemed very real to me. The old man evidently felt himself talking to some one.

'Yes, I suppose you're right,' said Graeme doubtfully; 'but there's a lot of stuff I can't swallow.'

'When you take medicine you don't swallow the bottle,' I replied, for his trouble was not mine.

'If I were sure of the medicine, I wouldn't mind the bottle, and yet it acts well enough,' he went on. 'I don't mind Lachlan; he's a Highland mystic, and has visions, and Sandy's almost as bad, and Baptiste is an impulsive little chap. Those don't count much. But old man Nelson is a cool-blooded, level-headed old fellow; has seen a lot of life, too. And then there's Craig. He has a better head than I have, and is as hot-blooded, and yet he is living and slaving away in that hole, and really enjoys it. There must be something in it.'

'Oh, look here, Graeme,' I burst out impatiently; 'what's the use of your talking like that? Of course there's something in it. I here's everything in it. The trouble with me is I can't face the music. It calls for a life where a fellow must go in for straight, steady work, self-denial, and that sort of thing; and I'm too Bohemian for that, and too lazy. But that fellow Craig makes one feel horribly uncomfortable.'

Graeme put his head on one side, and examined me curiously.

'I believe you're right about yourself. You always were a luxurious beggar. But that's not where it catches me.'

We sat and smoked and talked of other things for an hour, and then turned in. As I was dropping off I was roused by Graeme's voice--

'Are you going to the preparatory service on Friday night?'

'Don't know,' I replied rather sleepily.

'I say, do you remember the preparatory service at home?' There was something in his voice that set me wide awake.

'Yes. Rather terrific, wasn't it? But I always felt better after it,' I replied.

'To me'--he was sitting up in bed now--'to me it was like a call to arms, or rather like a call for a forlorn hope. None but volunteers wanted. Do you remember the thrill in the old governor's voice as he dared any but the right stuff to come on?'

'We'll go in on Friday night,' I said.

And so we did. Sandy took a load of men with his team, and Graeme and I drove in the light sleigh.

The meeting was in the church, and over a hundred men were present. There was some singing of familiar hymns at first, and then Mr. Craig read the same story as we had heard in the stable, that most perfect of all parables, the Prodigal Son. Baptiste nudged Sandy in delight, and whispered something, but Sandy held his face so absolutely expressionless that Graeme was moved to say--

'Look at Sandy! Did you ever see such a graven image? Something has hit him hard.'

The men were held fast by the story. The voice of the reader, low, earnest, and thrilling with the tender pathos of the tale, carried the words to our hearts, while a glance, a gesture, a movement of the body gave us the vision of it all as he was seeing it.

Then, in simplest of words, he told us what the story meant, holding us the while with eyes, and voice, and gesture. He compelled us scorn the gay, heartless selfishness of the young fool setting forth so jauntily from the broken home; he moved our pity and our sympathy for the young profligate, who, broken and deserted, had still pluck enough to determine to work his way back, and who, in utter desperation, at last gave it up; and then he showed us the homecoming--the ragged, heart-sick tramp, with hesitating steps, stumbling along the dusty road, and then the rush of the old father, his garments fluttering, and his voice heard in broken cries. I see and hear it all now, whenever the words are read.

He announced the hymn, 'Just as I am,' read the first verse, and then went on: 'There you are, men, every man of you, somewhere on the road. Some of you are too lazy'--here Graeme nudged me--'and some of you haven't got enough yet of the far country to come back. May there be a chance for you when you want to come! Men, you all want to go back home, and when you go you'll want to put on your soft clothes, and you won't go till you can go in good style; but where did the prodigal get his good clothes?' Quick came the answer in Baptiste's shrill voice--

'From de old fadder!'

No one was surprised, and the minister went on--

'Yes! and that's where we must get the good, clean heart, the good, clean, brave heart, from our Father. Don't wait, but, just as you are, come. Sing.'

They sang, not loud, as they would 'Stand Up,' or even 'The Sweet By and By,' but in voices subdued, holding down the power in them.

After the singing, Craig stood a moment gazing down at the men, and then said quietly--

'Any man want to come? You all might come. We all must come.' Then, sweeping his arm over the audience, and turning half round as if to move off, he cried, in a voice that thrilled to the heart's core--

'Oh! come on! Let's go back!'

The effect was overpowering. It seemed to me that the whole company half rose to their feet. Of the prayer that immediately followed, I only caught the opening sentence, 'Father, we are coming back,' for my attention was suddenly absorbed by Abe, the stage-driver, who was sitting next me. I could hear him swearing approval and admiration, saying to himself--

'Ain't he a clinker! I'll be gee-whizzly-gol-dusted if he ain't a malleable-iron-double-back-action self-adjusting corn-cracker.' And the prayer continued to be punctuated with like admiring and even more sulphurous expletives. It was an incongruous medley. The earnest, reverent prayer, and the earnest, admiring profanity, rendered chaotic one's ideas of religious propriety. The feelings in both were akin; the method of expression somewhat widely diverse.

After prayer, Craig's tone changed utterly. In a quiet, matter-of-fact, business-like way he stated his plan of organisation, and called for all who wished to join to remain after the benediction. Some fifty men were left, among them Nelson, Sandy, Lachlan Campbell, Baptiste, Shaw, Nixon, Geordie, and Billy Breen, who tried to get out, but was held fast by Geordie.

Graeme was passing out, but I signed him to remain, saying that I wished 'to see the thing out.' Abe sat still beside me, swearing disgustedly at the fellows 'who were going back on the preacher.' Craig appeared amazed at the number of men remaining, and seemed to fear that something was wrong. He put before them the terms of discipleship, as the Master put them to the eager scribe, and he did not make them easy. He pictured the kind of work to be done, and the kind of men needed for the doing of it. Abe grew uneasy as the minister went on to describe the completeness of the surrender, the intensity of the loyalty demanded.

'That knocks me out, I reckon,' he muttered, in a disappointed tone; 'I ain't up to that grade.' And as Craig described the heroism called for, the magnificence of the fight, the worth of it, and the outcome of it all, Abe ground out: I'll be blanked if I wouldn't like to take a hand, but I guess I'm not in it.' Craig finished by saying--

'I want to put this quite fairly. It is not any league of mine; you're not joining my company; it is no easy business, and it is for your whole life. What do you say? Do I put it fairly? What do you say, Nelson?'

Nelson rose slowly, and with difficulty began--

'I may be all wrong, but you made it easier for me, Mr. Craig. You said He would see me through, or I should never have risked it. Perhaps I am wrong,' and the old man looked troubled. Craig sprang up.

'No! no! Thank God, no! He will see every man through who will trust his life to Him. Every man, no matter how tough he is, no matter how broken.'

Then Nelson straightened himself up and said--

'Well, sir! I believe a lot of the men would go in for this if they were dead sure they would get through.'

'Get through!' said Craig; 'never a fear of it. It is a hard fight, a long fight, a glorious fight,' throwing up his head, but every man who squarely trusts Him, and takes Him as Lord and Master, comes out victor!'

'Bon!' said Baptiste 'Das me. You tink He's take me in dat fight, M'sieu Craig, heh?' His eyes were blazing.

'You mean it?' asked Craig almost sternly.

'Yes! by gar!' said the little Frenchman eagerly.

'Hear what He says, then'; and Craig, turning over the leaves of his Testament, read solemnly the words, 'Swear not at all.'

'Non! For sure! Den I stop him,' replied Baptiste earnestly; and Craig wrote his name down.

Poor Abe looked amazed and distressed, rose slowly, and saying, 'That jars my whisky jug,' passed out. There was a slight movement near the organ, and glancing up I saw Mrs. Mavor put her face hastily in her hands. The men's faces were anxious and troubled, and Nelson said in a voice that broke--

'Tell them what you told me, sir.' But Craig was troubled too, and replied, 'You tell them, Nelson!' and Nelson told the men the story of how he began just five weeks ago. The old man's voice steadied as he went on, and he grew eager as he told how he had been helped, and how the world was all different, and his heart seemed new. He spoke of his Friend as if He were some one that could be seen out at camp, that he knew well, and met every day.

But as he tried to say how deeply he regretted that he had not known all this years before, the old, hard face began to quiver, and the steady voice wavered. Then he pulled himself together, and said--

'I begin to feel sure He'll pull me through--me! the hardest man in the mountains! So don't you fear, boys. He's all right.'

Then the men gave in their names, one by one. When it came to Geordie's turn, he gave his name--

'George Crawford, frae the pairish o' Kilsyth, Scotland, an' ye'll juist pit doon the lad's name, Maister Craig; he's a wee bit fashed wi' the discoorse, but he has the root o' the maitter in him, I doot.' And so Billy Breen's name went down.

When the meeting was over, thirty-eight names stood upon the communion roll of the Black Rock Presbyterian Church; and it will ever be one of the regrets of my life that neither Graeme's name nor my own appeared on that roll. And two days after, when the cup went round on that first Communion Sabbath, from Nelson to Sandy, and from Sandy to Baptiste, and so on down the line to Billy Breen and Mrs. Mavor, and then to Abe, the driver, whom she had by her own mystic power lifted into hope and faith, I felt all the shame and pain of a traitor; and I believe, in my heart that the fire of that pain and shame burned something of the selfish cowardice out of me, and that it is burning still.

The last words of the minister, in the short address after the table had been served, were low, and sweet, and tender, but they were words of high courage; and before he had spoken them all, the men were listening with shining eyes, and when they rose to sing the closing hymn they stood straight and stiff like soldiers on parade.

And I wished more than ever I were one of them.

CHAPTER VIII
THE BREAKING OF THE LEAGUE

There is no doubt in my mind that nature designed me for a great painter. A railway director interfered with that design of nature, as he has with many another of hers, and by the transmission of an order for mountain pieces by the dozen, together with a cheque so large that I feared there was some mistake, he determined me to be an illustrator and designer for railway and like publications. I do not like these people ordering 'by the dozen.' Why should they not consider an artist's finer feelings? Perhaps they cannot understand them; but they understand my pictures, and I understand their cheques, and there we are quits. But so it came that I remained in Black Rock long enough to witness the breaking of the League.

Looking back upon the events of that night from the midst of gentle and decent surroundings, they now seem strangely unreal, but to me then they appeared only natural.

It was the Good Friday ball that wrecked the League. For the fact that the promoters of the ball determined that it should be a ball rather than a dance was taken by the League men as a concession to the new public opinion in favour of respectability created by the League. And when the manager's patronage had been secured (they failed to get Mrs. Mavor's), and it was further announced that, though held in the Black Rock Hotel ballroom--indeed, there was no other place--refreshments suited to the peculiar tastes of League men would be provided, it was felt to be almost a necessity that the League should approve, should indeed welcome, this concession to the public opinion in favour of respectability created by the League.

There were extreme men on both sides, of course. 'Idaho' Jack, professional gambler, for instance, frankly considered that the whole town was going to unmentionable depths of propriety. The organisation of the League was regarded by him, and by many others, as a sad retrograde towards the bondage of the ancient and dying East; and that he could not get drunk when and where he pleased, 'Idaho,' as he was called, regarded as a personal grievance.

But Idaho was never enamoured of the social ways of Black Rock. He was shocked and disgusted when he discovered that a 'gun' was decreed by British law to be an unnecessary adornment of a card-table. The manner of his discovery must have been interesting to behold.

It is said that Idaho was industriously pursuing his avocation in Slavin's, with his 'gun' lying upon the card-table convenient to his hand, when in walked policeman Jackson, her Majesty's sole representative in the Black Rock district. Jackson, 'Stonewall' Jackson, or 'Stonewall,' as he was called for obvious reasons, after watching the game for a few moments, gently tapped the pistol and asked what he used this for.

'I'll show you in two holy minutes if you don't light out,' said Idaho, hardly looking up, but very angrily, for the luck was against him. But Jackson tapped upon the table and said sweetly--

'You're a stranger here. You ought to get a guide-book and post yourself. Now, the boys know I don't interfere with an innocent little game, but there is a regulation against playing it with guns; so,' he added even more sweetly, but fastening Idaho with a look from his steel-grey eyes, 'I'll just take charge of this,' picking up the revolver; 'it might go off.'

Idaho's rage, great as it was, was quite swallowed up in his amazed disgust at the state of society that would permit such an outrage upon personal liberty. He was quite unable to play any more that evening, and it took several drinks all round to restore him to articulate speech. The rest of the night was spent in retailing for his instruction stories of the ways of Stonewall Jackson.

Idaho bought a new 'gun,' but he wore it 'in his clothes,' and used it chiefly in the pastime of shooting out the lights or in picking off the heels from the boys' boots while a stag dance was in progress in Slavin's. But in Stonewall's presence Idaho was a most correct citizen. Stonewall he could understand and appreciate. He was six feet three, and had an eye of unpleasant penetration. But this new feeling in the community for respectability he could neither understand nor endure. The League became the object of his indignant aversion, and the League men of his contempt. He had many sympathisers, and frequent were the assaults upon the newly-born sobriety of Billy Breen and others of the League. But Geordie's watchful care and Mrs. Mavor's steady influence, together with the loyal co-operation of the League men, kept Billy safe so far. Nixon, too, was a marked man. It may be that he carried himself with unnecessary jauntiness toward Slavin and Idaho, saluting the former with, 'Awful dry weather! eh, Slavin?' and the latter with, 'Hello, old sport! how's times?' causing them to swear deeply; and, as it turned out, to do more than swear.

But on the whole the anti-League men were in favour of a respectable ball, and most of the League men determined to show their appreciation of the concession of the committee to the principles of the League in the important matter of refreshments by attending in force.

Nixon would not go. However jauntily he might talk, he could not trust himself, as he said, where whisky was flowing, for it got into his nose 'like a fish-hook into a salmon.' He was from Nova Scotia. For like reason, Vernon Winton, the young Oxford fellow, would not go. When they chaffed, his lips grew a little thinner, and the colour deepened in his handsome face, but he went on his way. Geordie despised the 'hale hypothick' as a 'daft ploy,' and the spending of five dollars upon a ticket he considered a 'sinfu' waste o' guid siller'; and he warned Billy against 'coontenancin' ony sic redeeklus nonsense.'

But no one expected Billy to go; although the last two months he had done wonders for his personal appearance, and for his position in the social scale as well. They all knew what a fight he was making, and esteemed him accordingly. How well I remember the pleased pride in his face when he told me in the afternoon of the committee's urgent request that he should join the orchestra with his 'cello! It was not simply that his 'cello was his joy and pride, but he felt it to be a recognition of his return to respectability.

I have often wondered how things combine at times to a man's destruction.

Had Mr. Craig not been away at the Landing that week, had Geordie not been on the night-shift, had Mrs. Mavor not been so occupied with the care of her sick child, it may be Billy might have been saved his fall.

The anticipation of the ball stirred Black Rock and the camps with a thrill of expectant delight. Nowadays, when I find myself forced to leave my quiet smoke in my studio after dinner at the call of some social engagement which I have failed to elude, I groan at my hard lot, and I wonder as I look back and remember the pleasurable anticipation with which I viewed the approaching ball. But I do not wonder now any more than I did then at the eager delight of the men who for seven days in the week swung their picks up in the dark breasts of the mines, or who chopped and sawed among the solitary silences of the great forests. Any break in the long and weary monotony was welcome; what mattered the cost or consequence! To the rudest and least cultured of them the sameness of the life must have been hard to bear; but what it was to men who had seen life in its most cultured and attractive forms I fail to imagine. From the mine, black and foul, to the shack, bare, cheerless, and sometimes hideously repulsive, life swung in heart-grinding monotony till the longing for a 'big drink' or some other 'big break' became too great to bear.

It was well on towards evening when Sandy's four horse team, with a load of men from the woods, came swinging round the curves of the mountain-road and down the street. A gay crowd they were with their bright, brown faces and hearty voices; and in ten minutes the whole street seemed alive with lumbermen--they had a faculty of spreading themselves so. After night fell the miners came down 'done up slick,' for this was a great occasion, and they must be up to it. The manager appeared in evening dress; but this was voted 'too giddy' by the majority.

As Graeme and I passed up to the Black Rock Hotel, in the large store-room of which the ball was to be held, we met old man Nelson looking very grave.

'Going, Nelson, aren't you?' I said.

'Yes,' he answered slowly; 'I'll drop in, though I don't like the look of things much.'

'What's the matter, Nelson?' asked Graeme cheerily. 'There's no funeral on.'

'Perhaps not,' replied Nelson, 'but I wish Mr. Craig were home.' And then he added, 'There's Idaho and Slavin together, and you may bet the devil isn't far off.'

But Graeme laughed at his suspicion, and we passed on. The orchestra was tuning up. There were two violins, a concertina, and the 'cello. Billy Breen was lovingly fingering his instrument, now and then indulging himself in a little snatch of some air that came to him out of his happier past. He looked perfectly delighted, and as I paused to listen he gave me a proud glance out of his deep, little, blue eyes, and went on playing softly to himself. Presently Shaw came along.

'That's good, Billy,' he called out. 'You've got the trick yet, I see.'

But Billy only nodded and went on playing.

'Where's Nixon?' I asked.

'Gone to bed,' said Shaw, 'and I am glad of it. He finds that the safest place on pay-day afternoon. The boys don't bother him there.'

The dancing-room was lined on two sides with beer-barrels and whisky-kegs; at one end the orchestra sat, at the other was a table with refreshments, where the 'soft drinks' might be had. Those who wanted anything else might pass through a short passage into the bar just behind.

This was evidently a superior kind of ball, for the men kept on their coats, and went through the various figures with faces of unnatural solemnity. But the strain upon their feelings was quite apparent, and it became a question how long it could be maintained. As the trips through the passage-way became more frequent the dancing grew in vigour and hilarity, until by the time supper was announced the stiffness had sufficiently vanished to give no further anxiety to the committee.

But the committee had other cause for concern, inasmuch as after supper certain of the miners appeared with their coats off, and proceeded to 'knock the knots out of the floor' in break-down dances of extraordinary energy. These, however, were beguiled into the bar-room and 'filled up' for safety, for the committee were determined that the respectability of the ball should be preserved to the end. Their reputation was at stake, not in Black Rock only, but at the Landing as well, from which most of the ladies had come; and to be shamed in the presence of the Landing people could not be borne. Their difficulties seemed to be increasing, for at this point something seemed to go wrong with the orchestra. The 'cello appeared to be wandering aimlessly up and down the scale, occasionally picking up the tune with animation, and then dropping it. As Billy saw me approaching, he drew himself up with great solemnity, gravely winked at me, and said--

'Shlipped a cog, Mishter Connor! Mosh hunfortunate! Beauchiful hinstrument, but shlips a cog. Mosh hunfortunate!'

And he wagged his little head sagely, playing all the while for dear life, now second and now lead.

Poor Billy! I pitied him, but I thought chiefly of the beautiful, eager face that leaned towards him the night the League was made, and of the bright voice that said, 'You'll sign with me, Billy?' and it seemed to me a cruel deed to make him lose his grip of life and hope; for this is what the pledge meant to him.

While I was trying to get Billy away to some safe place, I heard a great shouting in the direction of the bar, followed by trampling and scuffling of feet in the passage-way. Suddenly a man burst through, crying--

'Let me go! Stand back! I know what I'm about!'

It was Nixon, dressed in his best; black clothes, blue shirt, red tie, looking handsome enough, but half-drunk and wildly excited. The highland Fling competition was on at the moment, and Angus Campbell, Lachlan's brother, was representing the lumber camps in the contest. Nixon looked on approvingly for a few moments, then with a quick movement he seized the little Highlander, swung him in his powerful arms clean off the floor, and deposited him gently upon a beer-barrel. Then he stepped into the centre of the room, bowed to the judges, and began a sailor's hornpipe.

The committee were perplexed, but after deliberation they decided to humour the new competitor, especially as they knew that Nixon with whisky in him was unpleasant to cross.

Lightly and gracefully he went through his steps, the men crowding in from the bar to admire, for Nixon was famed for his hornpipe. But when, after the hornpipe, he proceeded to execute a clog-dance, garnished with acrobatic feats, the committee interfered. There were cries of 'Put him out!' and 'Let him alone! Go on, Nixon!' And Nixon hurled back into the crowd two of the committee who had laid remonstrating hands upon him, and, standing in the open centre, cried out scornfully--

'Put me out! Put me out! Certainly! Help yourselves! Don't mind me!' Then grinding his teeth, so that I heard them across the room, he added with savage deliberation, 'If any man lays a finger on me, I'll--I'll eat his liver cold.'

He stood for a few moments glaring round upon the company, and then strode toward the bar, followed by the crowd wildly yelling. The ball was forthwith broken up. I looked around for Billy, but he was nowhere to be seen. Graeme touched my arm--

'There's going to be something of a time, so just keep your eyes skinned.'

'What are you going to do?' I asked.

'Do? Keep myself beautifully out of trouble,' he replied.

In a few moments the crowd came surging back headed by Nixon, who was waving a whisky-bottle over his head and yelling as one possessed.

'Hello!' exclaimed Graeme softly, 'I begin to see. Look there!'

'What's up?' I asked.

'You see Idaho and Slavin and their pets,' he replied.

'They've got poor Nixon in tow. Idaho is rather nasty,' he added, 'but I think I'll take a hand in this game; I've seen some of Idaho's work before.'

The scene was one quite strange to me, and was wild beyond description. A hundred men filled the room. Bottles were passed from hand to hand, and men drank their fill. Behind the refreshment-tables stood the hotelman and his bar-keeper with their coats off and sleeves rolled up to the shoulder, passing out bottles, and drawing beer and whisky from two kegs hoisted up for that purpose. Nixon was in his glory. It was his night. Every man was to get drunk at his expense, he proclaimed, flinging down bills upon the table. Near him were some League men he was treating liberally, and never far away were Idaho and Slavin passing bottles, but evidently drinking little.

I followed Graeme, not feeling too comfortable, for this sort of thing was new to me, but admiring the cool assurance with which he made his way through the crowd that swayed and yelled and swore and laughed in a most disconcerting man-ner.

'Hello!' shouted Nixon as he caught sight of Graeme. 'Here you are!' passing him a bottle. 'You're a knocker, a double-handed front door knocker. You polished off old whisky-soak here, old demijohn,' pointing to Slavin, 'and I'll lay five to one we can lick any blankety blank thieves in the crowd,' and he held up a roll of bills.

But Graeme proposed that he should give the hornpipe again, and the floor was cleared at once, for Nixon's hornpipe was very popular, and tonight, of course, was in high favour. In the midst of his dance Nixon stopped short, his arms dropped to his side, his face had a look of fear, of horror.

There, before him, in his riding-cloak and boots, with his whip in his hand as he had come from his ride, stood Mr. Craig. His face was pallid, and his dark eyes were blazing with fierce light. As Nixon stopped, Craig stepped forward to him, and sweeping his eyes round upon the circle he said in tones intense with scorn--

'You cowards! You get a man where he's weak! Cowards! you'd damn his soul for his money!'

There was dead silence, and Craig, lifting his hat, said solemnly--

'May God forgive you this night's work!'

Then, turning to Nixon, and throwing his arm over his shoulder, he said in a voice broken and husky--

'Come on, Nixon! we'll go!'

Idaho made a motion as if to stop him, but Graeme stepped quickly foreword and said sharply, 'Make way there, can't you?' and the crowd fell back and we four passed through, Nixon walking as in a dream, with Craig's arm about him. Down the street we went in silence, and on to Craig's shack, where we found old man Nelson, with the fire blazing, and strong coffee steaming on the stove. It was he that had told Craig, on his arrival from the Landing, of Nixon's fall.

There was nothing of reproach, but only gentlest pity, in tone and touch as Craig placed the half-drunk, dazed man in his easy-chair, took off his boots, brought him his own slippers, and gave him coffee. Then, as his stupor began to overcome him, Craig put him in his own bed, and came forth with a face written over with grief.

'Don't mind, old chap,' said Graeme kindly.

But Craig looked at him without a word, and, throwing himself into a chair, put his face in his hands. As we sat there in silence the door was suddenly pushed open and in walked Abe Baker with the words, 'Where is Nixon?' and we told him where he was. We were still talking when again a tap came to the door, and Shaw came in looking much disturbed.

'Did you hear about Nixon?' he asked. We told him what we knew.

'But did you hear how they got him?' he asked, excitedly.

As he told us the tale, the men stood listening, with faces growing hard.

It appeared that after the making of the League the Black Rock Hotel man had bet Idaho one hundred to fifty that Nixon could not be got to drink before Easter. All Idaho's schemes had failed, and now he had only three days in which to win his money, and the ball was his last chance. Here again he was balked, for Nixon, resisting all entreaties, barred his shack door and went to bed before nightfall, according to his invariable custom on pay-days. At midnight some of Idaho's men came battering at the door for admission, which Nixon reluctantly granted. For half an hour they used every art of persuasion to induce him to go down to the ball, the glorious success of which was glowingly depicted; but Nixon remained immovable, and they took their departure, baffled and cursing. In two hours they returned drunk enough to be dangerous, kicked at the door in vain, finally gained entrance through the window, hauled Nixon out of bed, and, holding a glass of whisky to his lips, bade him drink. But he knocked the glass sway, spilling the liquor over himself and the bed.

It was drink or fight, and Nixon was ready to fight; but after parley they had a drink all round, and fell to persuasion again. The night was cold, and poor Nixon sat shivering on the edge of his bed. If he would take one drink they would leave him alone. He need not show himself so stiff. The whisky fumes filled his nostrils. If one drink would get them off, surely that was better than fighting and killing some one or getting killed. He hesitated, yielded, drank his glass. They sat about him amiably drinking, and lauding him as a fine fellow after all. One more glass before they left. Then Nixon rose, dressed himself, drank all that was left of the bottle, put his money in his pocket, and came down to the dance, wild with his old-time madness, reckless of faith and pledge, forgetful of home, wife, babies, his whole being absorbed in one great passion--to drink and drink and drink till he could drink no more.

Before Shaw had finished his tale, Craig's eyes were streaming with tears, and groans of rage and pity broke alternately from him. Abe remained speechless for a time, not trusting himself; but as he heard Craig groan, 'Oh, the beasts! the fiends!' he seemed encouraged to let himself loose, and he began swearing with the coolest and most blood-curdling deliberation. Craig listened with evident approval, apparently finding complete satisfaction in Abe's performance, when suddenly he seemed to waken up, caught Abe by the arm, and said in a horror-stricken voice--

'Stop! stop! God forgive us! we must not swear like this.'

Abe stopped at once, and in a surprised and slightly grieved voice said--

'Why! what's the matter with that? Ain't that what you wanted?'

'Yes! yes! God forgive me! I am afraid it was,' he answered hurriedly; 'but I must not.'

'Oh, don't you worry,' went on Abe cheerfully; 'I'll look after that part; and anyway, ain't they the blankest blankety blank'--going off again into a roll of curses, till Craig, in an agony of entreaty, succeeded in arresting the flow of profanity possible to no one but a mountain stage-driver. Abe paused looking hurt, and asked if they did not deserve everything he was calling down upon them.

'Yes, yes,' urged Craig; 'but that is not our business.'

'Well! so I reckoned,' replied Abe, recognising the limitations of the cloth; 'you ain't used to it, and you can't be expected to do it; but it just makes me feel good--let out o' school like--to properly do 'em up, the blank, blank,' and off he went again.

It was only under the pressure of Mr. Craig's prayers and commands that he finally agreed 'to hold in, though it was tough.'

'What's to be done?' asked Shaw.

'Nothing,' answered Craig bitterly. He was exhausted with his long ride from the Landing, and broken with bitter disappointment over the ruin of all that he had laboured so long to accomplish.

'Nonsense,' said Graeme; 'there's a good deal to do.'

It was agreed that Craig should remain with Nixon while the others of us should gather up what fragments we could find of the broken League. We had just opened the door, when we met a man striding up at a great pace. It was Geordie Crawford.

'Hae ye seen the lad?' was his salutation. No one replied. So I told Geordie of my last sight of Billy in the orchestra.

'An' did ye no' gang aifter him?' he asked in indignant surprise, adding with some contempt, 'Man! but ye're a feckless buddie.'

'Billy gone too!' said Shaw. 'They might have let Billy alone.'

Poor Craig stood in a dumb agony. Billy's fall seemed more than he could bear. We went out, leaving him heart-broken amid the ruins of his League.

CHAPTER IX
THE LEAGUE'S REVENGE

As we stood outside of Craig's shack in the dim starlight, we could not hide from ourselves that we were beaten. It was not so much grief as a blind fury that filled my heart, and looking at the faces of the men about me I read the same feeling there. But what could we do? The yells of carousing miners down at Slavin's told us that nothing could be done with them that night. To be so utterly beaten, and unfairly, and with no chance of revenge, was maddening.

'I'd like to get back at 'em,' said Abe, carefully repressing himself.

'I've got it, men,' said Graeme suddenly. 'This town does not require all the whisky there is in it'; and he unfolded his plan. It was to gain possession of Slavin's saloon and the bar of the Black Rock Hotel, and clear out all the liquor to be found in both these places. I did not much like the idea; and Geordie said, 'I'm ga'en aifter the lad; I'll hae naethin' tae dae wi' yon. It's' no' that easy, an' it's a sinfu' waste.'

But Abe was wild to try it, and Shaw was quite willing, while old Nelson sternly approved.

'Nelson, you and Shaw get a couple of our men and attend to the saloon. Slavin and the whole gang are up at the Black Rock, so you won't have much trouble; but come to us as soon as you can.'

And so we went our ways.

Then followed a scene the like of which I can never hope to see again, and it was worth a man's seeing. But there were times that night when I wished I had not agreed to follow Graeme in his plot. As we went up to the hotel, I asked Graeme, 'What about the law of this?'

'Law!' he replied indignantly. 'They haven't troubled much about law in the whisky business here. They get a keg of high wines and some drugs and begin operations. No!' he went on; 'if we can get the crowd out, and ourselves in, we'll make them break the law in getting us out. The law won't trouble us over smuggled whisky. It will be a great lark, and they won't crow too loud over the League.'

I did not like the undertaking at first; but as I thought of the whole wretched illegal business flourishing upon the weakness of the men in the mines and camps, whom I had learned to regard as brothers, and especially as I thought of the cowards that did for Nixon, I let my scruples go, and determined, with Abe, 'to get back at 'em.'

We had no difficulty getting them out. Abe began to yell. Some men rushed out to learn the cause. He seized the foremost man, making a hideous uproar all the while, and in three minutes had every man out of the hotel and a lively row going on.

In two minutes more Graeme and I had the door to the ball-room locked and barricaded with empty casks. We then closed the door of the bar-room leading to the outside. The bar-room was a strongly built log-shack, with a heavy door secured, after the manner of the early cabins, with two strong oak bars, so that we felt safe from attack from that quarter.

The ball-room we could not hold long, for the door was slight and entrance was possible through the windows. But as only a few casks of liquor were left there, our main work would be in the bar, so that the fight would be to hold the passage-way. This we barricaded with casks and tables. But by this time the crowd had begun to realise what had happened, and were wildly yelling at door and windows. With an axe which Graeme had brought with him the casks were soon stove in, and left to empty themselves.

As I was about to empty the last cask, Graeme stopped me, saying, 'Let that stand here. It will help us.' And so it did. 'Now skip for the barricade,' yelled Graeme, as a man came crashing through the window. Before he could regain his feet, however, Graeme had seized him and flung him out upon the heads of the crowd outside. But through the other windows men were coming in, and Graeme rushed for the barricade, followed by two of the enemy, the foremost of whom I received at the top and hurled back upon the others.

'Now, be quick!' said Graeme; 'I'll hold this. Don't break any bottles on the floor--throw them out there,' pointing to a little window high up in the wall.

I made all haste. The casks did not take much time, and soon the whisky and beer were flowing over the floor. It made me think of Geordie's regret over the 'sinfu' waste.' The bottles took longer, and glancing up now and then I saw that Graeme was being hard pressed. Men would leap, two and three at a time, upon the barricade, and Graeme's arms would shoot out, and over they would topple upon the heads of those nearest. It was a great sight to see him standing alone with a smile on his face and the light of battle in his eye, coolly meeting his assailants with those terrific, lightning-like blows. In fifteen minutes my work was done.

'What next?' I asked. 'How do we get out?'

'How is the door?' he replied.

I looked through the port-hole and said, 'A crowd of men waiting.'

'We'll have to make a dash for it, I fancy,' he replied cheerfully, though his face was covered with blood and his breath was coming in short gasps.

'Get down the bars and be ready.' But even as he spoke a chair hurled from below caught him on the arm, and before he could recover, a man had cleared the barricade and was upon him like a tiger. It was Idaho Jack.

'Hold the barricade,' Graeme called out, as they both went down.

I sprang to his place, but I had not much hope of holding it long. I had the heavy oak bar of the door in my hands, and swinging it round my head I made the crowd give back for a few moments.

Meantime Graeme had shaken off his enemy, who was circling about him upon his tip-toes, with a long knife in his hand, waiting for a chance to spring.

'I have been waiting for this for some time, Mr. Graeme,' he said smiling.

'Yes,' replied Graeme, 'ever since I spoiled your cut-throat game in 'Frisco. How is the little one?' he added sarcastically.

Idaho's face lost its smile and became distorted with fury as he replied, spitting out his words, 'She--is--where you will be before I am done with you.'

'Ah! you murdered her too! You'll hang some beautiful day, Idaho,' said Graeme, as Idaho sprang upon him.

Graeme dodged his blow and caught his forearm with his left hand and held up high the murderous knife. Back and forward they swayed over the floor, slippery with whisky, the knife held high in the air. I wondered why Graeme did not strike, and then I saw his right hand hung limp from the wrist. The men were crowding upon the barricade. I was in despair. Graeme's strength was going fast. With a yell of exultant fury Idaho threw himself with all his weight upon Graeme, who could only cling to him. They swayed together towards me, but as they fell I brought down my bar upon the upraised hand and sent the knife flying across the room. Idaho's howl of rage and pain was mingled with a shout from below, and there, dashing the crowd right and left, came old Nelson, followed by Abe, Sandy, Baptiste, Shaw, and others. As they reached the barricade it crashed down and, carrying me with it, pinned me fast.

Looking out between the barrels, I saw what froze my heart with horror. In the fall Graeme had wound his arms about his enemy and held him in a grip so deadly that he could not strike; but Graeme's strength was failing, and when I looked I saw that Idaho was slowly dragging both across the slippery floor to where the knife lay. Nearer and nearer his outstretched fingers came to the knife. In vain I yelled and struggled. My voice was lost in the awful din, and the barricade held me fast. Above me, standing on a barrel-head, was Baptiste, yelling like a demon. In vain I called to him. My fingers could just reach his foot, and he heeded not at all my touch. Slowly Idaho was dragging his almost unconscious victim toward the knife. His fingers were touching the blade point, when, under a sudden inspiration, I pulled out my penknife, opened it with my teeth, and drove the blade into Baptiste's foot. With a blood-curdling yell he sprang down and began dancing round in his rage, peering among the barrels.

'Look! look!' I was calling in agony, and pointing; 'for heaven's sake, look! Baptiste!'

The fingers had closed upon the knife, the knife was already high in the air, when, with a shriek, Baptiste cleared the room at a bound, and, before the knife could fall, the little Frenchman's boot had caught the uplifted wrist, and sent the knife flying to the wall.

Then there was a great rushing sound as of wind through the forest, and the lights went out. When I awoke, I found myself lying with my head on Graeme's knees, and Baptiste sprinkling snow on my face. As I looked up Graeme leaned over me, and, smiling down into my eyes, he said--

'Good boy! It was a great fight, and we put it up well'; and then he whispered, 'I owe you my life, my boy.'

His words thrilled my heart through and through, for I loved him as only men can love men; but I only answered--

'I could not keep them back.'

'It was well done,' he said; and I felt proud. I confess I was thankful to be so well out of it, for Graeme got off with a bone in his wrist broken, and I with a couple of ribs cracked; but had it not been for the open barrel of whisky which kept them occupied for a time, offering too good a chance to be lost, and for the timely arrival of Nelson, neither of us had ever seen the light again.

We found Craig sound asleep upon his couch. His consternation on waking to see us torn, bruised, and bloody was laughable; but he hastened to find us warm water and bandages, and we soon felt comfortable.

Baptiste was radiant with pride and light over the fight, and hovered about Graeme and me giving vent to his feelings in admiring French and English expletives. But Abe was disgusted because of the failure at Slavin's; for when Nelson looked in, he saw Slavin's French-Canadian wife in charge, with her baby on her lap, and he came back to Shaw and said, 'Come away, we can't touch this'; and Shaw, after looking in, agreed that nothing could be done. A baby held the fort.

As Craig listened to the account of the fight, he tried hard not to approve, but he could not keep the gleam out of his eyes; and as I pictured Graeme dashing back the crowd thronging the barricade till he was brought down by the chair, Craig laughed gently, and put his hand on Graeme's knee. And as I went on to describe my agony while Idaho's fingers were gradually nearing the knife, his face grew pale and his eyes grew wide with horror.

'Baptiste here did the business,' I said, and the little Frenchman nodded complacently and said--

'Dat's me for sure.'

'By the way, how is your foot?' asked Graeme.

'He's fuss-rate. Dat's what you call--one bite of--of--dat leel bees, he's dere, you put your finger dere, he's not dere!--what you call him?'

'Flea!' I suggested.

'Oui!' cried Baptiste. 'Dat's one bite of flea.'

'I was thankful I was under the barrels,' I replied, smiling.

'Oui! Dat's mak' me ver mad. I jump an' swear mos' awful bad. Dat's pardon me, M'sieu Craig, heh?'

But Craig only smiled at him rather sadly. 'It was awfully risky,' he said to Graeme, 'and it was hardly worth it. They'll get more whisky, and anyway the League is gone.'

'Well,' said Graeme with a sigh of satisfaction, 'it is not quite such a one-sided affair as it was.'

And we could say nothing in reply, for we could hear Nixon snoring in the next room, and no one had heard of Billy, and there were others of the League that we knew were even now down at Slavin's. It was thought best that all should remain in Mr. Craig's shack, not knowing what might happen; and so we lay where we could and we needed none to sing us to sleep.

When I awoke, stiff and sore, it was to find breakfast ready and old man Nelson in charge. As we were seated, Craig came in, and I saw that he was not the man of the night before. His courage had come back, his face was quiet and his eye clear; he was his own man again.

'Geordie has been out all night, but has failed to find Billy,' he announced quietly.

We did not talk much; Graeme and I worried with our broken bones, and the others suffered from a general morning depression. But, after breakfast, as the men were beginning to move, Craig took down his Bible, and saying--

'Wait a few minutes, men!' he read slowly, in his beautiful clear voice, that psalm for all fighters--

'God is our refuge and strength,'

and soon to the noble words--

'The Lord of Hosts is with us;
The God of Jacob is our refuge.'

How the mighty words pulled us together, lifted us till we grew ashamed of our ignoble rage and of our ignoble depression!

And then Craig prayed in simple, straight-going words. There was acknowledgement of failure, but I knew he was thinking chiefly of himself; and there was gratitude, and that was for the men about him, and I felt my face burn with shame; and there was petition for help, and we all thought of Nixon, and Billy, and the men wakening from their debauch at Slavin's this pure, bright morning. And then he asked that we might be made faithful and worthy of God, whose battle it was. Then we all stood up and shook hands with him in silence, and every man knew a covenant was being made. But none saw his meeting with Nixon. He sent us all away before that.

Nothing was heard of the destruction of the hotel stock-in-trade. Unpleasant questions would certainly be asked, and the proprietor decided to let bad alone. On the point of respectability the success of the ball was not conspicuous, but the anti-League men were content, if not jubilant.

Billy Breen was found by Geordie late in the afternoon in his own old and deserted shack, breathing heavily, covered up in his filthy, mouldering bed-clothes, with a half-empty bottle of whisky at his side. Geordie's grief and rage were beyond even his Scotch control. He spoke few words, but these were of such concentrated vehemence that no one felt the need of Abe's assistance in vocabulary.

Poor Billy! We carried him to Mrs. Mavor's home; put him in a warm bath, rolled him in blankets, and gave him little sips of hot water, then of hot milk and coffee; as I had seen a clever doctor in the hospital treat a similar case of nerve and heart depression. But the already weakened system could not recover from the awful shock of the exposure following the debauch; and on Sunday afternoon we saw that his heart was failing fast. All day the miners had been dropping in to inquire after him, for Billy had been a great favourite in other days, and the attention of the town had been admiringly centred upon his fight of these last weeks. It was with no ordinary sorrow that the news of his condition was received. As Mrs. Mavor sang to him, his large coarse hands moved in time to the music, but he did not open his eyes till he heard Mr. Craig's voice in the next room; then he spoke his name, and Mr. Craig was kneeling beside him in a moment. The words came slowly--

'Oi tried--to fight it hout--but---oi got beaten. Hit 'urts to think 'E's hashamed o' me. Oi'd like t'a done better--oi would.'

'Ashamed of you, Billy!' said Craig, in a voice that broke. 'Not He.'

'An'--ye hall--'elped me so!' he went on. 'Oi wish oi'd 'a done better--oi do,' and his eyes sought Geordie, and then rested on Mrs. Mavor, who smiled back at him with a world of love in her eyes.

'You hain't hashamed o' me--yore heyes saigh so,' he said looking at her.

'No, Billy,' she said, and I wondered at her steady voice, 'not a bit. Why, Billy, I am proud of you.'

He gazed up at her with wonder and ineffable love in his little eyes, then lifted his hand slightly toward her. She knelt quickly and took it in both of hers, stroking it and kissing it.

'Oi haught t'a done better. Oi'm hawful sorry oi went back on 'Im. Hit was the lemonaide. The boys didn't mean no 'arm--but hit started the 'ell hinside.'

Geordie hurled out some bitter words.

'Don't be 'ard on 'em, Geordie; they didn't mean no 'arm,' he said, and his eyes kept waiting till Geordie said hurriedly--

'Na! na! lad--a'll juist leave them till the Almichty.'

Then Mrs. Mavor sang softly, smoothing his hand, 'Just as I am,' and Billy dozed quietly for half an hour.

When he awoke again his eyes turned to Mr. Craig, and they were troubled and anxious.

'Oi tried 'ard. Oi wanted to win,' he struggled to say. By this time Craig was master of himself, and he answered in a clear, distinct voice--

'Listen, Billy! You made a great fight, and you are going to win yet. And besides, do you remember the sheep that got lost over the mountains?'--this parable was Billy's special delight--'He didn't beat it when He got it, did he? He took it in His arms and carried it home. And so He will you.'

And Billy, keeping his eyes fastened on Mr. Craig, simply said--

'Will 'E?'

'Sure!' said Craig.

'Will 'E?' he repeated, turning his eyes upon Mrs. Mavor.

'Why, yes, Billy,' she answered cheerily, though the tears were streaming from her eyes. 'I would, and He loves you far more.'

He looked at her, smiled, and closed his eyes. I put my hand on his heart; it was fluttering feebly. Again a troubled look passed over his face.

'My--poor--hold--mother,' he whispered, 'she's--hin--the--wukus.'

'I shall take care of her, Billy,' said Mrs. Mavor, in a clear voice, and again Billy smiled. Then he turned his eyes to Mr. Craig, and from him to Geordie, and at last to Mrs. Mavor, where they rested. She bent over and kissed him twice on the forehead.

'Tell 'er,' he said, with difficulty, ''E's took me 'ome.'

'Yes, Billy!' she cried, gazing into his glazing eyes. He tried to lift her hand. She kissed him again. He drew one deep breath and lay quite still.

'Thank the blessed Saviour!' said Mr. Craig, reverently. 'He has taken him home.'

But Mrs. Mavor held the dead hand tight and sobbed out passionately, 'Oh, Billy, Billy! you helped me once when I needed help! I cannot forget!'

And Geordie, groaning, 'Ay, laddie, laddie,' passed out into the fading light of the early evening.

Next day no one went to work, for to all it seemed a sacred day. They carried him into the little church, and there Mr. Craig spoke of his long, hard fight, and of his final victory; for he died without a fear, and with love to the men who, not knowing, had been his death. And there was no bitterness in any heart, for Mr. Craig read the story of the sheep, and told how gently He had taken Billy home; but, though no word was spoken, it was there the League was made again.

They laid him under the pines, beside Lewis Mavor; and the miners threw sprigs of evergreen into the open grave. When Slavin, sobbing bitterly, brought his sprig, no one stopped him, though all thought it strange.

As we turned to leave the grave, the light from the evening sun came softly through the gap in the mountains, and, filling the valley, touched the trees and the little mound beneath with glory. And I thought of that other glory, which is brighter than the sun, and was not sorry that poor Billy's weary fight was over; and I could not help agreeing with Craig that it was there the League had its revenge.

CHAPTER X
WHAT CAME TO SLAVIN

Billy Breen's legacy to the Black Rock mining camp was a new League, which was more than the old League re-made. The League was new in its spirit and in its methods. The impression made upon the camp by Billy Breen's death was very remarkable, and I have never been quite able to account for it. The mood of the community at the time was peculiarly susceptible. Billy was one of the oldest of the old-timers. His decline and fall had been a long process, and his struggle for life and manhood was striking enough to arrest the attention and awaken the sympathy of the whole camp. We instinctively side with a man in his struggle for freedom; for we feel that freedom is native to him and to us. The sudden collapse of the struggle stirred the men with a deep pity for the beaten man, and a deep contempt for those who had tricked him to his doom. But though the pity and the contempt remained, the gloom was relieved and the sense of defeat removed from the men's minds by the transforming glory of Billy's last hour. Mr. Craig, reading of the tragedy of Billy's death, transfigured defeat into victory, and this was generally accepted by the men as the true reading, though to them it was full of mystery. But they could all understand and appreciate at full value the spirit that breathed through the words of the dying man: 'Don't be 'ard on 'em, they didn't mean no 'arm.' And this was the new spirit of the League.

It was this spirit that surprised Slavin into sudden tears at the grave's side. He had come braced for curses and vengeance, for all knew it was he who had doctored Billy's lemonade, and instead of vengeance the message from the dead that echoed through the voice of the living was one of pity and forgiveness.

But the days of the League's negative, defensive warfare were over. The fight was to the death, and now the war was to be carried into the enemy's country. The League men proposed a thoroughly equipped and well-conducted coffee-room, reading-room, and hall, to parallel the enemy's lines of operation, and defeat them with their own weapons upon their own ground. The main outlines of the scheme were clearly defined and were easily seen, but the perfecting of the details called for all Craig's tact and good sense. When, for instance, Vernon Winton, who had charge of the entertainment department, came for Craig's opinion as to a minstrel troupe and private theatricals, Craig was prompt with his answer--

'Anything clean goes.'

'A nigger show?' asked Winton.

'Depends upon the niggers,' replied Craig with a gravely comic look, shrewdly adding, 'ask Mrs. Mavor'; and so the League Minstrel and Dramatic Company became an established fact, and proved, as Craig afterwards told me, 'a great means of grace to the camp.'

Shaw had charge of the social department, whose special care it was to see that the men were made welcome to the cosy, cheerful reading room, where they might chat, smoke, read, write, or play games, according to fancy.

But Craig felt that the success or failure of the scheme would largely depend upon the character of the Resident Manager, who, while caring for reading-room and hall, would control and operate the important department represented by the coffee-room.

'At this point the whole business may come to grief,' he said to Mrs. Mavor, without whose counsel nothing was done.

'Why come to grief?' she asked brightly.

'Because if we don't get the right man, that's what will happen,' he replied in a tone that spoke of anxious worry.

'But we shall get the right man, never fear.' Her serene courage never faltered. 'He will come to us.'

Craig turned and gazed at her in frank admiration and said--

'If I only had your courage!'

'Courage!' she answered quickly. 'It is not for you to say that'; and at his answering look the red came into her cheek and the depths in her eyes glowed, and I marvelled and wondered, looking at Craig's cool face, whether his blood were running evenly through his veins. But his voice was quiet, a shade too quiet I thought, as he gravely replied--

'I would often be a coward but for the shame of it.'

And so the League waited for the man to come, who was to be Resident Manager and make the new enterprise a success. And come he did; but the manner of his coming was so extraordinary, that I have believed in the doctrine of a special providence ever since; for as Craig said, 'If he had come straight from Heaven I could not have been more surprised.'

While the League was thus waiting, its interest centred upon Slavin, chiefly because he represented more than any other the forces of the enemy; and though Billy Breen stood between him and the vengeance of the angry men who would have made short work of him and his saloon, nothing could save him from himself, and after the funeral Slavin went to his bar and drank whisky as he had never drunk before. But the more he drank the fiercer and gloomier he became, and when the men drinking with him chaffed him, he swore deeply and with such threats that they left him alone.

It did not help Slavin either to have Nixon stride in through the crowd drinking at his bar and give him words of warning.

'It is not your fault, Slavin,' he said in slow, cool voice, 'that you and your precious crew didn't sent me to my death, too. You've won your bet, but I want to say, that next time, though you are seven to one, or ten times that, when any of you boys offer me a drink I'll take you to mean fight, and I'll not disappoint you, and some one will be killed,' and so saying he strode out again, leaving a mean-looking crowd of men behind him. All who had not been concerned in the business at Nixon's shack expressed approval of his position, and hoped he would 'see it through.'

But the impression of Nixon's words upon Slavin was as nothing compared with that made by Geordie Crawford. It was not what he said so much as the manner of awful solemnity he carried. Geordie was struggling conscientiously to keep his promise to 'not be 'ard on the boys,' and found considerable relief in remembering that he had agreed 'to leave them tae the Almichty.' But the manner of leaving them was so solemnly awful, that I could not wonder that Slavin's superstitious Irish nature supplied him with supernatural terrors. It was the second day after the funeral that Geordie and I were walking towards Slavin's. There was a great shout of laughter as we drew near.

Geordie stopped short, and saying, 'We'll juist gang in a meenute,' passed through the crowd and up to the bar.

'Michael Slavin,' began Geordie, and the men stared in dead, silence, with their glasses in their hands. 'Michael Slavin, a' promised the lad a'd bear ye nae ill wull, but juist leave ye tae the Almichty; an' I want tae tell ye that a'm keepin' ma wur-r-d. But'--and here he raised his hand, and his voice became preternaturally solemn--'his bluid is upon yer han's. Do ye no' see it?'

His voice rose sharply, and as he pointed, Slavin instinctively glanced at his hands, and Geordie added--

'Ay, and the Lord will require it o' you and yer hoose.'

They told me that Slavin shivered as if taken with ague after Geordie went out, and though he laughed and swore, he did not stop drinking till he sank into a drunken stupor and had to be carried to bed. His little French-Canadian wife could not understand the change that had come over her husband.

'He's like one bear,' she confided to Mrs. Mavor, to whom she was showing her baby of a year old. 'He's not kees me one tam dis day. He's mos hawful bad, he's not even look at de baby.' And this seemed sufficient proof that something was seriously wrong; for she went on to say--

'He's tink more for dat leel baby dan for de whole worl'; he's tink more for dat baby dan for me,' but she shrugged her pretty little shoulders in deprecation of her speech.

'You must pray for him,' said Mrs. Mavor, 'and all will come right.'

'Ah! madame!' she replied earnestly, 'every day, every day, I pray la sainte Vierge et tous les saints for him.'

'You must pray to your Father in heaven for him.'

'Ah! oui! I weel pray,' and Mrs. Mavor sent her away bright with smiles, and with new hope and courage in her heart.

She had very soon need of all her courage, for at the week's end her baby fell dangerously ill. Slavin's anxiety and fear were not relieved much by the reports the men brought him from time to time of Geordie's ominous forebodings; for Geordie had no doubt but that the Avenger of Blood was hot upon Slavin's trail; and as the sickness grew, he became confirmed in this conviction. While he could not be said to find satisfaction in Slavin's impending affliction, he could hardly hide his complacency in the promptness of Providence in vindicating his theory of retribution.

But Geordie's complacency was somewhat rudely shocked by Mr. Craig's answer to his theory one day.

'You read your Bible to little profit, it seems to me, Geordie: or, perhaps, you have never read the Master's teaching about the Tower of Siloam. Better read that and take that warning to yourself.'

Geordie gazed after Mr. Craig as he turned away, and muttered--

'The toor o' Siloam, is it? Ay, a' ken fine aboot the toor o' Siloam, and aboot the toor o' Babel as weel; an' a've read, too, about the blaspheemious Herod, an' sic like. Man, but he's a hot-heided laddie, and lacks discreemeenation.'

'What about Herod, Geordie?' I asked.

'Aboot Herod?'--with a strong tinge of contempt in his tone. 'Aboot Herod? Man, hae ye no' read in the Screepturs aboot Herod an' the wur-r-ms in the wame o' him?'

'Oh yes, I see,' I hastened to answer.

'Ay, a fule can see what's flapped in his face,' with which bit of proverbial philosophy he suddenly left me. But Geordie thenceforth contented himself, in Mr. Craig's presence at least, with ominous head-shakings, equally aggravating, and impossible to answer.

That same night, however, Geordie showed that with all his theories he had a man's true heart, for he came in haste to Mrs. Mavor to say:

'Ye'll be needed ower yonder, a'm thinkin'.'

'Why? Is the baby worse? Have you been in?'

'Na, na,' replied Geordie cautiously, 'a'll no gang where a'm no wanted. But yon puir thing, ye can hear ootside weepin' and moanin'.'

'She'll maybe need ye tae,' he went on dubiously to me. 'Ye're a kind o' doctor, a' hear,' not committing himself to any opinion as to my professional value. But Slavin would have none of me, having got the doctor sober enough to prescribe.

The interest of the camp in Slavin was greatly increased by the illness of his baby, which was to him as the apple of his eye. There were a few who, impressed by Geordie's profound convictions upon the matter, were inclined to favour the retribution theory, and connect the baby's illness with the vengeance of the Almighty. Among these few was Slavin himself, and goaded by his remorseful terrors he sought relief in drink. But this brought him only deeper and fiercer gloom; so that between her suffering child and her savagely despairing husband, the poor mother was desperate with terror and grief.

'Ah! madame,' she sobbed to Mrs. Mavor, 'my heart is broke for him. He's heet noting for tree days, but jis dreenk, dreenk, dreenk.'

The next day a man came for me in haste. The baby was dying and the doctor was drunk. I found the little one in a convulsion lying across Mrs. Mavor's knees, the mother kneeling beside it, wringing her hands in a dumb agony, and Slavin standing near, silent and suffering. I glanced at the bottle of medicine upon the table and asked Mrs. Mavor the dose, and found the baby had been poisoned. My look of horror told Slavin something was wrong, and striding to me he caught my arm and asked--

'What is it? Is the medicine wrong?'

I tried to put him off, but his grip tightened till his fingers seemed to reach the bone.

'The dose is certainly too large; but let me go, I must do something.'

He let me go at once, saying in a voice that made my heart sore for him, 'He has killed my baby; he has killed my baby.' And then he cursed the doctor with awful curses, and with a look of such murderous fury on his face that I was glad the doctor was too drunk to appear.

His wife hearing his curses, and understanding the cause, broke out into wailing hard to bear.

'Ah! mon petit ange! It is dat wheeskey dat's keel mon baby. Ah! mon cheri, mon amour. Ah! mon Dieu! Ah, Michael, how often I say that wheeskey he's not good ting.'

It was more than Slavin could bear, and with awful curses he passed out. Mrs. Mavor laid the baby in its crib, for the convulsion had passed away; and putting her arms about the wailing little Frenchwoman, comforted and soothed her as a mother might her child.

'And you must help your husband,' I heard her say. 'He will need you more than ever. Think of him.'

'Ah oui! I weel,' was the quick reply, and from that moment there was no more wailing.

It seemed no more than a minute till Slavin came in again, sober, quiet, and steady; the passion was all gone from his face, and only the grief remained.

As we stood leaning over the sleeping child the little thing opened its eyes, saw its father, and smiled. It was too much for him. The big man dropped on his knees with a dry sob.

'Is there no chance at all, at all?' he whispered, but I could give him no hope. He immediately rose, and pulling himself together, stood perfectly quiet.

A new terror seized upon the mother.

'My baby is not--what you call it?' going through the form of baptism. 'An' he will not come to la sainte Vierge,' she said, crossing herself.

'Do not fear for your little one,' said Mrs. Mavor, still with her arms about her. 'The good Saviour will take your darling into His own arms.'

But the mother would not be comforted by this. And Slavin too, was uneasy.

'Where is Father Goulet?' he asked.

'Ah! you were not good to the holy pere de las tam, Michael,' she replied sadly. 'The saints are not please for you.'

'Where is the priest?' he demanded.

'I know not for sure. At de Landin', dat's lak.'

'I'll go for him,' he said. But his wife clung to him, beseeching him not to leave her, and indeed he was loth to leave his little one.

I found Craig and told him the difficulty. With his usual promptness, he was ready with a solution.

'Nixon has a team. He will go.' Then he added, 'I wonder if they would not like me to baptize their little one. Father Goulet and I have exchanged offices before now. I remember how he came to one of my people in my absence, when she was dying, read with her, prayed with her, comforted her, and helped her across the river. He is a good soul, and has no nonsense about him. Send for me if you think there is need. It will make no difference to the baby, but it will comfort the mother.'

Nixon was willing enough to go; but when he came to the door Mrs. Mavor saw the hard look in his face. He had not forgotten his wrong, for day by day he was still fighting the devil within that Slavin had called to life. But Mrs. Mavor, under cover of getting him instructions, drew him into the room. While listening to her, his eyes wandered from one to the other of the group till they rested upon the little white face in the crib. She noticed the change in his face.

'They fear the little one will never see the Saviour if it is not baptized,' she said, in a low tone.

He was eager to go.

'I'll do my best to get the priest,' he said, and was gone on his sixty miles' race with death.

The long afternoon wore on, but before it was half gone I saw Nixon could not win, and that the priest would be too late, so I sent for Mr. Craig. From the moment he entered the room he took command of us all. He was so simple, so manly, so tender, the hearts of the parents instinctively turned to him.

As he was about to proceed with the baptism, the mother whispered to Mrs. Mavor, who hesitatingly asked Mr. Craig if he would object to using holy water.

'To me it is the same as any other,' he replied gravely.

'An' will he make the good sign?' asked the mother timidly.

And so the child was baptized by the Presbyterian minister with holy water and with the sign of the cross. I don't suppose it was orthodox, and it rendered chaotic some of my religious notions, but I thought more of Craig that moment than ever before. He was more man than minister, or perhaps he was so good a minister that day because so much a man. As he read about the Saviour and the children and the disciples who tried to get in between them, and as he told us the story in his own simple and beautiful way, and then went on to picture the home of the little children, and the same Saviour in the midst of them, I felt my heart grow warm, and I could easily understand the cry of the mother--

'Oh, mon Jesu, prenez moi aussi, take me wiz mon mignon.'

The cry wakened Slavin's heart, and he said huskily--

'Oh! Annette! Annette!'

'Ah, oui! an' Michael too!' Then to Mr. Craig--

'You tink He's tak me some day? Eh?'

'All who love Him,' he replied.

'An' Michael too?' she asked, her eyes searching his face, 'An' Michael too?'

But Craig only replied: 'All who love Him.'

'Ah, Michael, you must pray le bon Jesu. He's garde notre mignon.' And then she bent over the babe, whispering--

'Ah, mon cheri, mon amour, adieu! adieu! mon ange!' till Slavin put his arms about her and took her away, for as she was whispering her farewells, her baby, with a little answering sigh, passed into the House with many rooms.

'Whisht, Annette darlin'; don't cry for the baby,' said her husband. 'Shure it's better off than the rest av us, it is. An' didn't ye hear what the minister said about the beautiful place it is? An' shure he wouldn't lie to us at all.' But a mother cannot be comforted for her first-born son.

An hour later Nixon brought Father Goulet. He was a little Frenchman with gentle manners and the face of a saint. Craig welcomed him warmly, and told him what he had done.

'That is good, my brother,' he said, with gentle courtesy, and, turning to the mother, 'Your little one is safe.'

Behind Father Goulet came Nixon softly, and gazed down upon the little quiet face, beautiful with the magic of death. Slavin came quietly and stood beside him. Nixon turned and offered his hand. But Slavin said, moving slowly back--

'I did ye a wrong, Nixon, an' it's a sorry man I am this day for it.'

'Don't say a word, Slavin,' answered Nixon, hurriedly. 'I know how you feel. I've got a baby too. I want to see it again. That's why the break hurt me so.'

'As God's above,' replied Slavin earnestly, 'I'll hinder ye no more.' They shook hands, and we passed out.

We laid the baby under the pines, not far from Billy Breen, and the sweet spring wind blew through the Gap, and came softly down the valley, whispering to the pines and the grass and the hiding flowers of the New Life coming to the world. And the mother must have heard the whisper in her heart, for, as the Priest was saying the words of the Service, she stood with Mrs. Mavor's arms about her, and her eyes were looking far away beyond the purple mountain-tops, seeing what made her smile. And Slavin, too, looked different. His very features seemed finer. The coarseness was gone out of his face. What had come to him I could not tell.

But when the doctor came into Slavin's house that night it was the old Slavin I saw, but with a look of such deadly fury on his face that I tried to get the doctor out at once. But he was half drunk and after his manner was hideously humorous.

'How do, ladies! How do, gentlemen!' was his loud-voiced salutation. 'Quite a professional gathering, clergy predominating. Lion and Lamb too, ha! ha! which is the lamb, eh? ha! ha! very good! awfully sorry to hear of your loss, Mrs. Slavin; did our best you know, can't help this sort of thing.'

Before any one could move, Craig was at his side, and saying in a clear, firm voice, 'One moment, doctor,' caught him by the arm and had him out of the room before he knew it. Slavin, who had been crouching in his chair with hands twitching and eyes glaring, rose and followed, still crouching as he walked. I hurried after him, calling him back. Turning at my voice, the doctor saw Slavin approaching. There was something so terrifying in his swift noiseless crouching motion, that the doctor, crying out in fear 'Keep him off,' fairly turned and fled. He was too late. Like a tiger Slavin leaped upon him and without waiting to strike had him by the throat with both hands, and bearing him to the ground, worried him there as a dog might a cat.

Immediately Craig and I were upon him, but though we lifted him clear off the ground we could not loosen that two-handed strangling grip. At we were struggling there a light hand touched my shoulder. It was Father Goulet.

'Please let him go, and stand away from us,' he said, waving us back. We obeyed. He leaned over Slavin and spoke a few words to him. Slavin started as if struck a heavy blow, looked up at the priest with fear in his face, but still keeping his grip.

'Let him go,' said the priest. Slavin hesitated. 'Let him go! quick!' said the priest again, and Slavin with a snarl let go his hold and stood sullenly facing the priest.

Father Goulet regarded him steadily for some seconds and then asked--

'What would you do?' His voice was gentle enough, even sweet, but there was something in it that chilled my marrow. 'What would you do?' he repeated.

'He murdered my child,' growled Slavin.

'Ah! how?'

'He was drunk and poisoned him.'

'Ah! who gave him drink? Who made him a drunkard two years ago? Who has wrecked his life?'

There was no answer, and the even-toned voice went relentlessly on--

'Who is the murderer of your child now?'

Slavin groaned and shuddered.

'Go!' and the voice grew stern. 'Repent of your sin and add not another.'

Slavin turned his eyes upon the motionless figure on the ground and then upon the priest. Father Goulet took one step towards him, and, stretching out his hand and pointing with his finger, said--

'Go!'

And Slavin slowly backed away and went into his house. It was an extraordinary scene, and it is often with me now: the dark figure on the ground, the slight erect form of the priest with outstretched arm and finger, and Slavin backing away, fear and fury struggling in his face.

It was a near thing for the doctor, however, and two minutes more of that grip would have done for him. As it was, we had the greatest difficulty in reviving him.

What the priest did with Slavin after getting him inside I know not; that has always been a mystery to me. But when we were passing the saloon that night after taking Mrs. Mavor home, we saw a light and heard strange sounds within. Entering, we found another whisky raid in progress, Slavin himself being the raider. We stood some moments watching him knocking in the heads of casks and emptying bottles. I thought he had gone mad, and approached him cautiously.

'Hello, Slavin!' I called out; 'what does this mean?'

He paused in his strange work, and I saw that his face, though resolute, was quiet enough.

'It means I'm done wid the business, I am,' he said, in a determined voice. 'I'll help no more to kill any man, or,' in a lower tone, 'any man's baby.' The priest's words had struck home.

'Thank God, Slavin!' said Craig, offering his hand; 'you are much too good a man for the business.'

'Good or bad, I'm done wid it,' he replied, going on with his work.

'You are throwing away good money, Slavin,' I said, as the head of a cask crashed in.

'It's meself that knows it, for the price of whisky has riz in town this week,' he answered, giving me a look out of the corner of his eye. 'Bedad! it was a rare clever job,' referring to our Black Rock Hotel affair.

'But won't you be sorry for this?' asked Craig.

'Beloike I will; an' that's why I'm doin' it before I'm sorry for it,' he replied, with a delightful bull.

'Look here, Slavin,' said Craig earnestly; 'if I can be of use to you in any way, count on me.'

'It's good to me the both of yez have been, an' I'll not forget it to yez,' he replied, with like earnestness.

As we told Mrs. Mavor that night, for Craig thought it too good to keep, her eyes seemed to grow deeper and the light in them to glow more intense as she listened to Craig pouring out his tale. Then she gave him her hand and said--

'You have your man at last.'

'What man?'

'The man you have been waiting for.'

'Slavin!'

'Why not?'

'I never thought of it.'

'No more did he, nor any of us.' Then, after a pause, she added gently, 'He has been sent to us?'

'Do you know, I believe you are right,' Craig said slowly, and then added, 'But you always are.'

'I fear not,' she answered; but I thought she liked to hear his words.

The whole town was astounded next morning when Slavin went to work in the mines, and its astonishment only deepened as the days went on, and he stuck to his work. Before three weeks had gone the League had bought and remodelled the saloon and had secured Slavin as Resident Manager.

The evening of the reopening of Slavin's saloon, as it was still called, was long remembered in Black Rock. It was the occasion of the first appearance of 'The League Minstrel and Dramatic Troupe,' in what was described as a 'hair-lifting tragedy with appropriate musical selections.' Then there was a grand supper and speeches and great enthusiasm, which reached its climax when Nixon rose to propose the toast of the evening--'Our Saloon.' His speech was simply a quiet, manly account of his long struggle with the deadly enemy. When he came to speak of his recent defeat he said--

'And while I am blaming no one but myself, I am glad to-night that this saloon is on our side, for my own sake and for the sake of those who have been waiting long to see me. But before I sit down I want to say that while I live I shall not forget that I owe my life to the man that took me that night to his own shack and put me in his own bed, and met me next morning with an open hand; for I tell you I had sworn to God that that morning would be my last.'

Geordie's speech was characteristic. After a brief reference to the 'mysteerious ways o' Providence,' which he acknowledged he might sometimes fail to understand, he went on to express his unqualified approval of the new saloon.

'It's a cosy place, an' there's nae sulphur aboot. Besides a' that,' he went on enthusiastically, 'it'll be a terrible savin'. I've juist been coontin'.'

'You bet!' ejaculated a voice with great emphasis.

'I've juist been coontin',' went on Geordie, ignoring the remark and the laugh which followed, 'an' it's an awfu'-like money ye pit ower wi' the whusky. Ye see ye canna dae wi' ane bit glass; ye maun hae twa or three at the verra least, for it's no verra forrit ye get wi' ane glass. But wi' yon coffee ye juist get a saxpence-worth an' ye want nae mair.'

There was another shout of laughter, which puzzled Geordie much.

'I dinna see the jowk, but I've slippit ower in whusky mair nor a hunner dollars.'

Then he paused, looking hard before him, and twisting his face into extraordinary shapes till the men looked at him in wonder.

'I'm rale glad o' this saloon, but it's ower late for the lad that canna be helpit the noo. He'll not be needin' help o' oors, I doot, but there are ithers'--and he stopped abruptly and sat down, with no applause following.

But when Slavin, our saloon-keeper, rose to reply, the men jumped up on the seats and yelled till they could yell no more. Slavin stood, evidently in trouble with himself, and finally broke out--

'It's spacheless I am entirely. What's come to me I know not, nor how it's come. But I'll do my best for yez.' And then the yelling broke out again.

I did not yell myself. I was too busy watching the varying lights in Mrs. Mavor's eyes as she looked from Craig to the yelling men on the benches and tables, and then to Slavin, and I found myself wondering if she knew what it was that came to Slavin.

CHAPTER XI
THE TWO CALLS

With the call to Mr. Craig I fancy I had something to do myself. The call came from a young congregation in an eastern city, and was based partly upon his college record and more upon the advice of those among the authorities who knew his work in the mountains. But I flatter myself that my letters to friends who were of importance in that congregation were not without influence, for I was of the mind that the man who could handle Black Rock miners as he could was ready for something larger than a mountain mission. That he would refuse I had not imagined, though I ought to have known him better. He was but little troubled over it. He went with the call and the letters urging his acceptance to Mrs. Mavor. I was putting the last touches to some of my work in the room at the back of Mrs. Mavor's house when he came in. She read the letters and the call quietly, and waited for him to speak.

'Well?' he said; 'should I go?'

She started, and grew a little pale. His question suggested a possibility that had not occurred to her. That he could leave his work in Black Rock she had hitherto never imagined; but there was other work, and he was fit for good work anywhere. Why should he not go? I saw the fear in her face, but I saw more than fear in her eyes, as for a moment or two she let them rest upon Craig's face. I read her story, and I was not sorry for either of them. But she was too much a woman to show her heart easily to the man she loved, and her voice was even and calm as she answered his question.

'Is this a very large congregation?'

'One of the finest in all the East,' I put in for him. 'It will be a great thing for Craig.'

Craig was studying her curiously. I think she noticed his eyes upon her, for she went on even more quietly--

'It will be a great chance for work, and you are able for a larger sphere, you know, than poor Black Rock affords.'

'Who will take Black Rock?' he asked.

'Let some other fellow have a try at it,' I said. 'Why should you waste your talents here?'

'Waste?' cried Mrs. Mavor indignantly.

'Well, "bury," if you like it better,' I replied.

'It would not take much of a grave for that funeral,' said Craig, smiling.

'Oh,' said Mrs. Mavor, 'you will be a great man I know, and perhaps you ought to go now.'

But he answered coolly: 'There are fifty men wanting that Eastern charge, and there is only one wanting Black Rock, and I don't think Black Rock is anxious for a change, so I have determined to stay where I am yet a while.'

Even my deep disgust and disappointment did not prevent me from seeing the sudden leap of joy in Mrs. Mavor's eyes, but she, with a great effort, answered quietly--

'Black Rock will be very glad, and some of us very, very glad.'

Nothing could change his mind. There was no one he knew who could take his place just now, and why should he quit his work? It annoyed me considerably to feel he was right. Why is it that the right things are so frequently unpleasant?

And if I had had any doubt about the matter next Sabbath evening would have removed it. For the men came about him after the service and let him feel in their own way how much they approved his decision, though the self-sacrifice involved did not appeal to them. They were too truly Western to imagine that any inducements the East could offer could compensate for his loss of the West. It was only fitting that the West should have the best, and so the miners took almost as a matter of course, and certainly as their right, that the best man they knew should stay with them. But there were those who knew how much of what most men consider worth while he had given up, and they loved him no less for it.

Mrs. Mavor's call was not so easily disposed of. It came close upon the other, and stirred Black Rock as nothing else had ever stirred it before.

I found her one afternoon gazing vacantly at some legal documents spread out before her on the table, and evidently overcome by their contents. There was first a lawyer's letter informing her that by the death of her husband's father she had come into the whole of the Mavor estates, and all the wealth pertaining thereto. The letter asked for instructions, and urged an immediate return with a view to a personal superintendence of the estates. A letter, too, from a distant cousin of her husband urged her immediate return for many reasons, but chiefly on account of the old mother who had been left alone with none nearer of kin than himself to care for her and cheer her old age.

With these two came another letter from her mother-in-law herself. The crabbed, trembling characters were even more eloquent than the words with which the letter closed.

'I have lost my boy, and now my husband is gone, and I am a lonely woman. I have many servants, and some friends, but none near to me, none so near and dear as my dead son's wife. My days are not to be many. Come to me, my daughter; I want you and Lewis's child.'

'Must I go?' she asked with white lips.

'Do you know her well?' I asked.

'I only saw her once or twice,' she answered; 'but she has been very good to me.'

'She can hardly need you. She has friends. And surely you are needed here.'

She looked at me eagerly.

'Do you think so?' she said.

'Ask any man in the camp--Shaw, Nixon, young Winton, Geordie. Ask Craig,' I replied.

'Yes, he will tell me,' she said.

Even as she spoke Craig came up the steps. I passed into my studio and went on with my work, for my days at Black Rock were getting few, and many sketches remained to be filled in.

Through my open door I saw Mrs. Mavor lay her letters before Mr. Craig, saying, 'I have a call too.' They thought not of me.

He went through the papers, carefully laid them down without a word while she waited anxiously, almost impatiently, for him to speak.

'Well?' she asked, using his own words to her; 'should I go?'

'I do not know,' he replied; 'that is for you to decide--you know all the circumstances.'

'The letters tell all.' Her tone carried a feeling of disappointment. He did not appear to care.

'The estates are large?' he asked.

'Yes, large enough--twelve thousand a year.'

'And has your mother-in-law any one with her?'

'She has friends, but, as she says, none near of kin. Her nephew looks after the works--iron works, you know--he has shares in them.'

'She is evidently very lonely,' he answered gravely.

'What shall I do?' she asked, and I knew she was waiting to hear him urge her to stay; but he did not see, or at least gave no heed.

'I cannot say,' he repeated quietly. 'There are many things to consider; the estates--'

'The estates seem to trouble you,' she replied, almost fretfully. He looked up in surprise. I wondered at his slowness.

'Yes, the estates,' he went on, 'and tenants, I suppose--your mother-in-law, your little Marjorie's future, your own future.'

'The estates are in capable hands, I should suppose,' she urged, 'and my future depends upon what I choose my work to be.'

'But one cannot shift one's responsibilities,' he replied gravely. 'These estates, these tenants, have come to you, and with them come duties.'

'I do not want them,' she cried.

'That life has great possibilities of good,' he said kindly.

'I had thought that perhaps there was work for me here,' she suggested timidly.

'Great work,' he hastened to say. 'You have done great work. But you will do that wherever you go. The only question is where your work lies.'

'You think I should go,' she said suddenly and a little bitterly.

'I cannot bid you stay,' he answered steadily.

'How can I go?' she cried, appealing to him. 'Must I go?'

How he could resist that appeal I could not understand. His face was cold and hard, and his voice was almost harsh as he replied--

'If it is right, you will go--you must go.'

Then she burst forth--

'I cannot go. I shall stay here. My work is here; my heart is here. How can I go? You thought it worth your while to stay here and work, why should not I?'

The momentary gleam in his eyes died out, and again he said coldly--

'This work was clearly mine. I am needed here.'

'Yes, yes!' she cried, her voice full of pain; 'you are needed, but there is no need of me.'

'Stop, stop!' he said sharply; 'you must not say so.'

'I will say it, I must say it,' she cried, her voice vibrating with the intensity of her feeling. 'I know you do not need me; you have your work, your miners, your plans; you need no one; you are strong. But,' and her voice rose to a cry, 'I am not strong by myself; you have made me strong. I came here a foolish girl, foolish and selfish and narrow. God sent me grief. Three years ago my heart died. Now I am living again. I am a woman now, no longer a girl. You have done this for me. Your life, your words, yourself--you have showed me a better, a higher life, than I had ever known before, and now you send me away.'

She paused abruptly.

'Blind, stupid fool!' I said to myself.

He held himself resolutely in hand, answering carefully, but his voice had lost its coldness and was sweet and kind.

'Have I done this for you? Then surely God has been good to me. And you have helped me more than any words could tell you.'

'Helped!' she repeated scornfully.

'Yes, helped,' he answered, wondering at her scorn.

'You can do without my help,' she went on. 'You make people help you. You will get many to help you; but I need help, too.' She was standing before him with her hands tightly clasped; her face was pale, and her eyes deeper than ever. He sat looking up at her in a kind of maze as she poured out her words hot and fast.

'I am not thinking of you.' His coldness had hurt her deeply. 'I am selfish; I am thinking of myself. How shall I do? I have grown to depend on you, to look to you. It is nothing to you that I go, but to me--' She did not dare to finish.

By this time Craig was standing before her, his face deadly pale. When she came to the end of her words, he said, in a voice low, sweet, and thrilling with emotion--

'Ah, if you only knew! Do not make me forget myself. You do not guess what you are doing.'

'What am I doing? What is there to know, but that you tell me easily to go? She was struggling with the tears she was too proud to let him see.

He put his hands resolutely behind him, looking at her as if studying her face for the first time. Under his searching look she dropped her eyes, and the warm colour came slowly up into her neck and face; then, as if with a sudden resolve, she lifted her eyes to his, and looked back at him unflinchingly.

He started, surprised, drew slowly near, put his hands upon her shoulders, surprise giving place to wild joy. She never moved her eyes; they drew him towards her. He took her face between his hands, smiled into her eyes, kissed her lips. She did not move; he stood back from her, threw up his head, and laughed aloud. She came to him, put her head upon his breast, and lifting up her face said, 'Kiss me.' He put his arms about her, bent down and kissed her lips again, and then reverently her brow. Then putting her back from him, but still holding both her hands, he cried--

'Not you shall not go. I shall never let you go.'

She gave a little sigh of content, and, smiling up at him, said--

'I can go now'; but even as she spoke the flush died from her face, and she shuddered.

'Never!' he almost shouted; 'nothing shall take you away. We shall work here together.'

'Ah, if we could, if we only could,' she said piteously.

'Why not?' he demanded fiercely.

'You will send me away. You will say it is right for me to go,' she replied sadly.

'Do we not love each other?' was his impatient answer.

'Ah! yes, love,' she said; 'but love is not all.'

'No!' cried Craig; 'but love is the best'

'Yes!' she said sadly; 'love is the best, and it is for love's sake we will do the best.'

'There is no better work than here. Surely this is best,' and he pictured his plans before her. She listened eagerly.

'Oh! if it should be right,' she cried, 'I will do what you say. You are good, you are wise, you shall tell me.'

She could not have recalled him better. He stood silent some moments, then burst out passionately--

'Why then has love come to us? We did not seek it. Surely love is of God. Does God mock us?'

He threw himself into his chair, pouring out his words of passionate protestation. She listened, smiling, then came to him and, touching his hair as a mother might her child's, said--

'Oh, I am very happy! I was afraid you would not care, and I could not bear to go that way.'

'You shall not go,' he cried aloud, as if in pain. 'Nothing can make that right.'

But she only said, 'You shall tell me to-morrow. You cannot see to-night, but you will see, and you will tell me.'

He stood up and, holding both her hands, looked long into her eyes, then turned abruptly away and went out.

She stood where he left her for some moments, her face radiant, and her hands pressed upon her heart. Then she came toward my room. She found me busy with my painting, but as I looked up and met her eyes she flushed slightly, and said--

'I quite forgot you.'

'So it appeared to me.'

'You heard?'

'And saw,' I replied boldly. 'It would have been rude to interrupt, you see.'

'Oh, I am so glad and thankful.'

'Yes; it was rather considerate of me.'

'Oh, I don't mean that,' the flush deepening; 'I am glad you know.'

'I have known some time.'

'How could you? I only knew to-day myself.'

'I have eyes.' She flushed again.

'Do you mean that people--' she began anxiously.

'No; I am not "people." I have eyes, and my eyes have been opened.'

'Opened?'

'Yes, by love.'

Then I told her openly how, weeks ago, I struggled with my heart and mastered it, for I saw it was vain to love her, because she loved a better man who loved her in return. She looked at me shyly and said--

'I am sorry.'

'Don't worry,' I said cheerfully. 'I didn't break my heart, you know; I stopped it in time.'

'Oh!' she said, slightly disappointed; then her lips began to twitch, and she went off into a fit of hysterical laughter.

'Forgive me,' she said humbly; 'but you speak as if it had been a fever.'

'Fever is nothing to it,' I said solemnly. 'It was a near thing.' At which she went off again. I was glad to see her laugh. It gave me time to recover my equilibrium, and it relieved her intense emotional strain. So I rattled on some nonsense about Craig and myself till I saw she was giving no heed, but thinking her own thoughts: and what these were it was not hard to guess.

Suddenly she broke in upon my talk--

'He will tell me that I must go from him.'

'I hope he is no such fool,' I said emphatically and somewhat rudely, I fear; for I confess I was impatient with the very possibility of separation for these two, to whom love meant so much. Some people take this sort of thing easily and some not so easily; but love for a woman like this comes once only to a man, and then he carries it with him through the length of his life, and warms his heart with it in death. And when a man smiles or sneers at such love as this, I pity him, and say no word, for my speech would be in an unknown tongue. So my heart was sore as I sat looking up at this woman who stood before me, overflowing with the joy of her new love, and dully conscious of the coming pain. But I soon found it was vain to urge my opinion that she should remain and share the work and life of the man she loved. She only answered--

'You will help him all you can, for it will hurt him to have me go.'

The quiver in her voice took out all the anger from my heart, and before I knew I had pledged myself to do all I could to help him.

But when I came upon him that night, sitting in the light of his fire, I saw he must be let alone. Some battles we fight side by side, with comrades cheering us and being cheered to victory; but there are fights we may not share, and these are deadly fights where lives are lost and won. So I could only lay my hand upon his shoulder without a word. He looked up quickly, read my face, and said, with a groan--

'You know?'

'I could not help it. But why groan?'

'She will think it right to go,' he said despairingly.

'Then you must think for her; you must bring some common-sense to bear upon the question.'

'I cannot see clearly yet,' he said; 'the light will come.'

'May I show you how I see it?' I asked.

'Go on,' he said.

For an hour I talked; eloquently, even vehemently urging the reason and right of my opinion. She would be doing no more than every woman does, no more than she did before; her mother-in-law had a comfortable home, all that wealth could procure, good servants, and friends; the estates could be managed without her personal supervision; after a few years' work here they would go east for little Majorie's education; why should two lives be broken?--and so I went on.

He listened carefully, even eagerly.

'You make a good case,' he said, with a slight smile. 'I will take time. Perhaps you are right. The light will come. Surely it will come. But,' and here he sprang up and stretched his arms to full length above his head, 'I am not sorry; whatever comes I am not sorry. It is great to have her love, but greater to love her as I do. Thank God! nothing can take that away. I am willing, glad to suffer for the joy of loving her.'

Next morning, before I was awake, he was gone, leaving a note for me:--

'MY DEAR CONNOR,--I am due at the Landing. When I see you again I think my way will be clear. Now all is dark. At times I am a coward, and often, as you sometimes kindly inform me, an ass; but I hope I may never become a mule.

I am willing to be led, or want to be, at any rate. I must do the best--not second best--for her, for me. The best only is God's will. What else would you have? Be good to her these days, dear old fellow.--Yours, CRAIG.'

How often those words have braced me he will never know, but I am a better man for them: 'The best only is God's will. What else would you have?' I resolved I would rage and fret no more, and that I would worry Mrs. Mavor with no more argument or expostulation, but, as my friend had asked, 'Be good to her.'

CHAPTER XII
LOVE IS NOT ALL

Those days when we were waiting Craig's return we spent in the woods or on the mountain sides, or down in the canyon beside the stream that danced down to meet the Black Rock river, I talking and sketching and reading, and she listening and dreaming, with often a happy smile upon her face. But there were moments when a cloud of shuddering fear would sweep the smile away, and then I would talk of Craig till the smile came back again.

But the woods and the mountains and the river were her best, her wisest, friends during those days. How sweet the ministry of the woods to her! The trees were in their new summer leaves, fresh and full of life. They swayed and rustled above us, flinging their interlacing shadows upon us, and their swaying and their rustling soothed and comforted like the voice and touch of a mother. And the mountains, too, in all the glory of their varying robes of blues and purples, stood calmly, solemnly about us, uplifting our souls into regions of rest. The changing lights and shadows flitted swiftly over their rugged fronts, but left them ever as before in their steadfast majesty. 'God's in His heaven.' What would you have? And ever the little river sang its cheerful courage, fearing not the great mountains that threatened to bar its passage to the sea. Mrs. Mavor heard the song and her courage rose.

'We too shall find our way,' she said, and I believed her.

But through these days I could not make her out, and I found myself studying her as I might a new acquaintance. Years had fallen from her; she was a girl again, full of young warm life. She was as sweet as before, but there was a soft shyness over her, a half-shamed, half-frank consciousness in her face, a glad light in her eyes that made her all new to me. Her perfect trust in Craig was touching to see.

'He will tell me what to do,' she would say, till I began to realise how impossible it would be for him to betray such trust, and be anything but true to the best.

So much did I dread Craig's home-coming, that I sent for Graeme and old man Nelson, who was more and more Graeme's trusted counsellor and friend. They were both highly excited by the story I had to tell, for I thought it best to tell them all;

but I was not a little surprised and disgusted that they did not see the matter in my light. In vain I protested against the madness of allowing anything to send these two from each other. Graeme summed up the discussion in his own emphatic way, but with an earnestness in his words not usual with him.

'Craig will know better than any of us what is right to do, and he will do that, and no man can turn him from it; and,' he added, 'I should be sorry to try.'

Then my wrath rose, and I cried--

'It's a tremendous shame! They love each other. You are talking sentimental humbug and nonsense!'

'He must do the right,' said Nelson in his deep, quiet voice.

'Right! Nonsense! By what right does he send from him the woman he loves?'

'"He pleased not Himself,"' quoted Nelson reverently.

'Nelson is right,' said Graeme. 'I should not like to see him weaken.'

'Look here,' I stormed; 'I didn't bring you men to back him up in his nonsense. I thought you could keep your heads level.'

'Now, Connor,' said Graeme, 'don't rage--leave that for the heathen; it's bad form, and useless besides. Craig will walk his way where his light falls; and by all that's holy, I should hate to see him fail; for if he weakens like the rest of us my North Star will have dropped from my sky.'

'Nice selfish spirit,' I muttered.

'Entirely so. I'm not a saint, but I feel like steering by one when I see him.'

When after a week had gone, Craig rode up one early morning to his shack door, his face told me that he had fought his fight and had not been beaten. He had ridden all night and was ready to drop with weariness.

'Connor, old boy,' he said, putting out his hand; 'I'm rather played. There was a bad row at the Landing. I have just closed poor Colley's eyes. It was awful. I must get sleep. Look after Dandy, will you, like a good chap?'

'Oh, Dandy be hanged,!' I said, for I knew it was not the fight, nor the watching, nor the long ride that had shaken his iron nerve and given him that face. 'Go in and lie down I'll bring you something.'

'Wake me in the afternoon,' he said; 'she is waiting. Perhaps you will go to her'--his lips quivered--'my nerve is rather gone.' Then with a very wan smile he added, 'I am giving you a lot of trouble.'

'You go to thunder!' I burst out, for my throat was hot and sore with grief for him.

'I think I'd rather go to sleep,' he replied, still smiling. I could not speak, and was glad of the chance of being alone with Dandy.

When I came in I found him sitting with his head in his arms upon the table fast asleep. I made him tea, forced him to take a warm bath, and sent him to bed, while I went to Mrs. Mavor. I went with a fearful heart, but that was because I had forgotten the kind of woman she was.

She was standing in the light of the window waiting for me. Her face was pale but steady, there was a proud light in her fathomless eyes, a slight smile parted her lips, and she carried her head like a queen.

'Come in,' she said. 'You need not fear to tell me. I saw him ride home. He has not failed, thank God! I am proud of him; I knew he would be true. He loves me'-- she drew in her breath sharply, and a faint colour tinged her cheek--'but he knows love is not all--ah, love is not all! Oh! I am glad and proud!'

'Glad!' I gasped, amazed.

'You would not have him prove faithless!' she said with proud defiance.

'Oh, it is high sentimental nonsense,' I could not help saying.

'You should not say so,' she replied, and her voice rang clear. 'Honour, faith, and duty are sentiments, but they are not nonsense.'

In spite of my rage I was lost in amazed admiration of the high spirit of the woman who stood up so straight before me. But, as I told how worn and broken he was, she listened with changing colour and swelling bosom, her proud courage all gone, and only love, anxious and pitying, in her eyes.

'Shall I go to him?' she asked with timid eagerness and deepening colour.

'He is sleeping. He said he would come to you,' I replied.

'I shall wait for him,' she said softly, and the tenderness in her tone went straight to my heart, and it seemed to me a man might suffer much to be loved with love such as this.

In the early afternoon Graeme came to her. She met him with both hands out-stretched, saying in a low voice--

'I am very happy.'

'Are you sure?' he asked anxiously.

'Oh, yes,' she said, but her voice was like a sob; 'quite, quite sure.'

They talked long together till I saw that Craig must soon be coming, and I called Graeme away. He held her hands, looking steadily into her eyes and said--

'You are better even than I thought; I'm going to be a better man.'

Her eyes filled with tears, but her smile did not fade as she answered--

'Yes! you will be a good man, and God will give you work to do.'

He bent his head over her hands and stepped back from her as from a queen, but he spoke no word till we came to Craig's door. Then he said with humility that seemed strange in him, 'Connor, that is great, to conquer oneself. It is worth while. I am going to try.'

I would not have missed his meeting with Craig. Nelson was busy with tea. Craig was writing near the window. He looked up as Graeme came in, and nodded an easy good-evening; but Graeme strode to him and, putting one hand on his shoulder, held out his other for Craig to take.

After a moment's surprise, Craig rose to his feet, and, facing him squarely, took the offered hand in both of his and held it fast without a word. Graeme was the first to speak, and his voice was deep with emotion--

'You are a great man, a good man. I'd give something to have your grit.'

Poor Craig stood looking at him, not daring to speak for some moments, then he said quietly--

'Not good nor great, but, thank God, not quite a traitor.'

'Good man!' went on Graeme, patting him on the shoulder. 'Good man! But it's tough.'

Craig sat down quickly, saying, 'Don't do that, old chap!'

I went up with Craig to Mrs. Mavor's door. She did not hear us coming, but stood near the window gazing up at the mountains. She was dressed in some rich soft stuff, and wore at her breast a bunch of wild-flowers. I had never seen her so beautiful. I did not wonder that Craig paused with his foot upon the threshold to look at her. She turned and saw us. With a glad cry, 'Oh! my darling; you have come to me,' she came with outstretched arms. I turned and fled, but the cry and the vision were long with me.

It was decided that night that Mrs. Mavor should go the next week. A miner and his wife were going east, and I too would join the party.

The camp went into mourning at the news; but it was understood that any display of grief before Mrs. Mavor was bad form. She was not to be annoyed.

But when I suggested that she should leave quietly, and avoid the pain of saying good-bye, she flatly refused--

'I must say good-bye to every man. They love me and I love them.'

It was decided, too, at first, that there should be nothing in the way of a testimonial, but when Craig found out that the men were coming to her with all sorts of extraordinary gifts, he agreed that it would be better that they should unite in one gift. So it was agreed that I should buy a ring for her. And were it not that the contributions were strictly limited to one dollar, the purse that Slavin handed her when Shaw read the address at the farewell supper would have been many times filled with the gold that was pressed upon the committee. There were no speeches at the supper, except one by myself in reply on Mrs. Mavor's behalf. She had given me the words to say, and I was thoroughly prepared, else I should not have got through. I began in the usual way: 'Mr. Chairman, ladies and gentlemen, Mrs. Mavor is--' but I got no further, for at the mention of her name the men stood on the chairs and yelled until they could yell no more. There were over two hundred and fifty of them, and the effect was overpowering. But I got through my speech. I remember it well. It began--

'Mrs. Mavor is greatly touched by this mark of your love, and she will wear your ring always with pride.' And it ended with--

'She has one request to make, that you will be true to the League, and that you stand close about the man who did most to make it. She wishes me to say that however far away she may have to go, she is leaving her heart in Black Rock, and she can think of no greater joy than to come back to you again.'

Then they had 'The Sweet By and By,' but the men would not join in the refrain, unwilling to lose a note of the glorious voice they loved to hear. Before the last verse she beckoned to me. I went to her standing by Craig's side as he played for her. 'Ask them to sing,' she entreated; 'I cannot bear it.'

'Mrs. Mavor wishes you to sing in the refrain,' I said, and at once the men sat up and cleared their throats. The singing was not good, but at the first sound of the hoarse notes of the men Craig's head went down over the organ, for he was thinking I suppose of the days before them when they would long in vain for that thrilling voice that soared high over their own hoarse tones. And after the voices died away he kept on playing till, half turning toward him, she sang alone once more the refrain in a voice low and sweet and tender, as if for him alone. And so he took it, for he smiled up at her his old smile full of courage and full of love.

Then for one whole hour she stood saying good-bye to those rough, gentle-hearted men whose inspiration to goodness she had been for five years. It was very wonderful and very quiet. It was understood that there was to be no nonsense, and Abe had been heard to declare that he would 'throw out any cotton-backed fool who couldn't hold himself down,' and further, he had enjoined them to remember that 'her arm wasn't a pump-handle.'

At last they were all gone, all but her guard of honour--Shaw, Vernon Winton, Geordie, Nixon, Abe, Nelson, Craig, and myself.

This was the real farewell; for, though in the early light of the next morning two hundred men stood silent about the stage, and then as it moved out waved their hats and yelled madly, this was the last touch they had of her hand. Her place was up on the driver's seat between Abe and Mr. Craig, who held little Marjorie on his knee. The rest of the guard of honour were to follow with Graeme's team. It was Winton's fine sense that kept Graeme from following them close. 'Let her go out alone,' he said, and so we held back and watched her go.

She stood with her back towards Abe's plunging four-horse team, and steadying herself with one hand on Abe's shoulder, gazed down upon us. Her head was bare, her lips parted in a smile, her eyes glowing with their own deep light; and so, facing us, erect and smiling, she drove away, waving us farewell till Abe swung his team into the canyon road and we saw her no more. A sigh shuddered through the crowd, and, with a sob in his voice, Winton said: 'God help us all.'

I close my eyes and see it all again. The waving crowd of dark-faced men, the plunging horses, and, high up beside the driver, the swaying, smiling, waving figure, and about all the mountains, framing the picture with their dark sides and white peaks tipped with the gold of the rising sun. It is a picture I love to look upon, albeit it calls up another that I can never see but through tears.

I look across a strip of ever-widening water, at a group of men upon the wharf, standing with heads uncovered, every man a hero, though not a man of them suspects it, least of all the man who stands in front, strong, resolute, self-conquered.

And, gazing long, I think I see him turn again to his place among the men of the mountains, not forgetting, but every day remembering the great love that came to him, and remembering, too, that love is not all. It is then the tears come.

But for that picture two of us at least are better men to-day.

CHAPTER XIII
HOW NELSON CAME HOME

Through the long summer the mountains and the pines were with me. And through the winter, too, busy as I was filling in my Black Rock sketches for the railway people who would still persist in ordering them by the dozen, the memory of that stirring life would come over me, and once more I would be among the silent pines and the mighty snow-peaked mountains. And before me would appear the red-shirted shantymen or dark-faced miners, great, free, bold fellows, driving me almost mad with the desire to seize and fix those swiftly changing groups of picturesque figures. At such times I would drop my sketch, and with eager brush seize a group, a face, a figure, and that is how my studio comes to be filled with the men of Black Rock. There they are all about me. Graeme and the men from the woods, Sandy, Baptiste, the Campbells, and in many attitudes and groups old man Nelson; Craig, too, and his miners, Shaw, Geordie, Nixon, and poor old Billy and the keeper of the League saloon.

It seemed as if I lived among them, and the illusion was greatly helped by the vivid letters Graeme sent me from time to time. Brief notes came now and then from Craig too, to whom I had sent a faithful account of how I had brought Mrs. Mavor to her ship, and of how I had watched her sail away with none too brave a face, as she held up her hand that bore the miners' ring, and smiled with that deep light in her eyes. Ah! those eyes have driven me to despair and made me fear that I am no great painter after all, in spite of what my friends tell me who come in to smoke my good cigars and praise my brush. I can get the brow and hair, and mouth and pose, but the eyes! the eyes elude me--and the faces of Mrs. Mavor on my wall, that the men praise and rave over, are not such as I could show to any of the men from the mountains.

Graeme's letters tell me chiefly about Craig and his doings, and about old man Nelson; while from Craig I hear about Graeme, and how he and Nelson are standing at his back, and doing what they can to fill the gap that never can be filled. The three are much together, I can see, and I am glad for them all, but chiefly for Craig, whose face, grief-stricken but resolute, and often gentle as a woman's, will not leave me nor let me rest in peace.

The note of thanks he sent me was entirely characteristic. There were no heroics, much less pining or self-pity. It was simple and manly, not ignoring the pain but making much of the joy. And then they had their work to do. That note, so clear, so manly, so nobly sensible, stiffens my back yet at times.

In the spring came the startling news that Black Rock would soon be no more. The mines were to close down on April 1. The company, having allured the confiding public with enticing descriptions of marvellous drifts, veins, assays, and prospects, and having expended vast sums of the public's money in developing the mines till the assurance of their reliability was absolutely final, calmly shut down and vanished. With their vanishing vanishes Black Rock, not without loss and much deep cursing on the part of the men brought some hundreds of miles to aid the company in its extraordinary and wholly inexplicable game.

Personally it grieved me to think that my plan of returning to Black Rock could never be carried out. It was a great compensation, however, that the three men most representative to me of that life were soon to visit me actually in my own home and den. Graeme's letter said that in one month they might be expected to appear. At least he and Nelson were soon to come, and Craig would soon follow.

On receiving the great news, I at once looked up young Nelson and his sister, and we proceeded to celebrate the joyful prospect with a specially good dinner. I found the greatest delight in picturing the joy and pride of the old man in his children, whom he had not seen for fifteen or sixteen years. The mother had died some five years before, then the farm was sold, and the brother and sister came into the city; and any father might be proud of them. The son was a well-made young fellow, handsome enough, thoughtful, and solid-looking. The girl reminded me of her father. The same resolution was seen in mouth and jaw, and the same passion slumbered in the dark grey eyes. She was not beautiful, but she carried herself well, and one would always look at her twice. It would be worth something to see the meeting between father and daughter.

But fate, the greatest artist of us all, takes little count of the careful drawing and the bright colouring of our fancy's pictures, but with rude hand deranges all, and with one swift sweep paints out the bright and paints in the dark. And this trick he served me when, one June night, after long and anxious waiting for some word from the west, my door suddenly opened and Graeme walked in upon me like a spectre, grey and voiceless. My shout of welcome was choked back by the look in his face, and I could only gaze at him and wait for his word. He gripped my hand, tried to speak, but failed to make words come.

'Sit down, old man,' I said, pushing, him into my chair, 'and take your time.'

He obeyed, looking up at me with burning, sleepless eyes. My heart was sore for his misery, and I said: 'Don't mind, old chap; it can't be so awfully bad. You're here safe and sound at any rate,' and so I went on to give him time. But he shuddered and looked round and groaned.

'Now look here, Graeme, let's have it. When did you land here? Where is Nelson? Why didn't you bring him up?'

'He is at the station in his coffin,' he answered slowly.

'In his coffin?' I echoed, my beautiful pictures all vanishing. 'How was it?'

'Through my cursed folly,' he groaned bitterly.

'What happened?' I asked. But ignoring my question, he said: 'I must see his children. I have not slept for four nights. I hardly know what I am doing; but I can't rest till I see his children. I promised him. Get them for me.'

'To-morrow will do. Go to sleep now, and we shall arrange everything to-morrow,' I urged.

'No!' he said fiercely; 'to-night--now!'

In half an hour they were listening, pale and grief-stricken, to the story of their father's death.

Poor Graeme was relentless in his self-condemnation as he told how, through his 'cursed folly,' old Nelson was killed. The three, Craig, Graeme, and Nelson, had come as far as Victoria together. There they left Craig, and came on to San Francisco. In an evil hour Graeme met a companion of other and evil days, and it was not long till the old fever came upon him.

In vain Nelson warned and pleaded. The reaction from the monotony and poverty of camp life to the excitement and luxury of the San Francisco gaming palaces swung Graeme quite off his feet, and all that Nelson could do was to follow from place to place and keep watch.

'And there he would sit,' said Graeme in a hard, bitter voice, 'waiting and watching often till the grey morning light, while my madness held me fast to the table. One night,' here he paused a moment, put his face in his hands and shuddered; but quickly he was master of himself again, and went on in the same hard voice--'One night my partner and I were playing two men who had done us up before. I knew they were cheating, but could not detect them. Game after game they won, till I was furious at my stupidity in not being able to catch them. Happening to glance at Nelson in the corner, I caught a meaning look, and looking again, he threw me a signal. I knew at once what the fraud was, and next game charged the fellow with it. He gave me the lie; I struck his mouth, but before I could draw my gun, his partner had me by the arms. What followed I hardly know. While I was struggling to get free, I saw him reach for his weapon; but, as he drew it, Nelson sprang across the table, and bore him down. When the row was ever, three men lay on the floor. One was Nelson; he took the shot meant for me.'

Again the story paused.

'And the man that shot him?'

I started at the intense fierceness in the voice, and, looking upon the girl, saw her eyes blazing with a terrible light.

'He is dead,' answered Graeme indifferently.

'You killed him?' she asked eagerly.

Graeme looked at her curiously, and answered slowly--

'I did not mean to. He came at me. I struck him harder than I knew. He never moved.'

She drew a sigh of satisfaction, and waited.

'I got him to a private ward, had the best doctor in the city, and sent for Craig to Victoria. For three days we thought he would live--he was keen to get home; but by the time Craig came we had given up hope. Oh, but I was thankful to see Craig come in, and the joy in the old man's eyes was beautiful to see. There was no pain at last, and no fear. He would not allow me to reproach myself, saying over and over, "You would have done the same for me"--as I would, fast enough--"and it is better me than you. I am old and done; you will do much good yet for the boys." And he kept looking at me till I could only promise to do my best.

'But I am glad I told him how much good he had done me during the last year, for he seemed to think that too good to be true. And when Craig told him how he had helped the boys in the camp, and how Sandy and Baptiste and the Campbells would always be better men for his life among them, the old man's face actually shone, as if light were coming through. And with surprise and joy he kept on saying, "Do you think so? Do you think so? Perhaps so, perhaps so." At the last he talked of Christmas night at the camp. You were there, you remember. Craig had been holding a service, and something happened, I don't know what, but they both knew.'

'I know,' I said, and I saw again the picture of the old man under the pine, upon his knees in the snow, with his face turned up to the stars.

'Whatever it was, it was in his mind at the very last, and I can never forget his face as he turned it to Craig. One hears of such things: I had often, but had never put much faith in them; but joy, rapture, triumph, these are what were in his face, as he said, his breath coming short, "You said--He wouldn't--fail me--you were right--not once--not once--He stuck to me--I'm glad he told me--thank God--for you--you showed--me--I'll see Him--and--tell Him--" And Craig, kneeling beside him so steady--I was behaving like a fool--smiled down through his streaming tears into the dim eyes so brightly, till they could see no more. Thank him for that! He helped the old man through, and he helped me too, that night, thank God!' And Graeme's voice, hard till now, broke in a sob.

He had forgotten us, and was back beside his passing friend, and all his self-control could not keep back the flowing tears.

'It was his life for mine,' he said huskily.

The brother and sister were quietly weeping, but spoke no word, though I knew Graeme was waiting for them.

I took up the word, and told of what I had known of Nelson, and his influence upon the men of Black Rock. They listened eagerly enough, but still without speaking. There seemed nothing to say, till I suggested to Graeme that he must get some rest. Then the girl turned to him, and, impulsively putting out her hand, said--

'Oh, it is all so sad; but how can we ever thank you?'

'Thank me!' gasped Graeme. 'Can you forgive me? I brought him to his death.'

'No, no! You must not say so,' she answered hurriedly. 'You would have done the same for him.'

'God knows I would,' said Graeme earnestly; 'and God bless you for your words!' And I was thankful to see the tears start in his dry, burning eyes.

We carried him to the old home in the country, that he might lie by the side of the wife he had loved and wronged. A few friends met us at the wayside station, and followed in sad procession along the country road, that wound past farms and through woods, and at last up to the ascent where the quaint, old wooden church, black with the rains and snows of many years, stood among its silent graves. The little graveyard sloped gently towards the setting sun, and from it one could see, far on every side, the fields of grain and meadowland that wandered off over softly undulating hills to meet the maple woods at the horizon, dark, green, and cool. Here and there white farmhouses, with great barns standing near, looked out from clustering orchards.

Up the grass-grown walk, and through the crowding mounds, over which waves, uncut, the long, tangling grass, we bear our friend, and let him gently down into the kindly bosom of mother earth, dark, moist, and warm. The sound of a distant cowbell mingles with the voice of the last prayer; the clods drop heavily with heart-startling echo; the mound is heaped and shaped by kindly friends, sharing with one another the task; the long rough sods are laid over and patted into place; the old minister takes farewell in a few words of gentle sympathy; the brother and sister, with lingering looks at the two graves side by side, the old and the new, step into the farmer's carriage, and drive away; the sexton locks the gate and goes home, and we are left outside alone.

Then we went back and stood by Nelson's grave.

After a long silence Graeme spoke.

'Connor, he did not grudge his life to me--and I think'--and here the words came slowly--'I understand now what that means, "Who loved me and gave Himself for me."'

Then taking off his hat, he said reverently, 'By God's help Nelson's life shall not end, but shall go on. Yes, old man!' looking down upon the grave, 'I'm with you'; and lifting up his face to the calm sky, 'God help me to be true.'

Then he turned and walked briskly away, as one might who had pressing business, or as soldiers march from a comrade's grave to a merry tune, not that they have forgotten, but they have still to fight.

And this was the way old man Nelson came home.

CHAPTERS XIV.
GRAEME'S NEW BIRTH

There was more left in that grave than old man Nelson's dead body. It seemed to me that Graeme left part, at least, of his old self there, with his dead friend and comrade, in the quiet country churchyard. I waited long for the old careless, reckless spirit to appear, but he was never the same again. The change was unmistakable, but hard to define. He seemed to have resolved his life into a definite purpose. He was hardly so comfortable a fellow to be with; he made me feel even more lazy and useless than was my wont; but I respected him more, and liked him none the less. As a lion he was not a success. He would not roar. This was disappointing to me, and to his friends and mine, who had been waiting his return with eager expectation of tales of thrilling and bloodthirsty adventure.

His first days were spent in making right, or as nearly right as he could, the break that drove him to the west. His old firm (and I have had more respect for the humanity of lawyers ever since) behaved really well. They proved the restoration of their confidence in his integrity and ability by offering him a place in the firm, which, however, he would not accept. Then, when he felt clean, as he said, he posted off home, taking me with him. During the railway journey of four hours he hardly spoke; but when we had left the town behind, and had fairly got upon the country road that led toward the home ten miles away, his speech came to him in a great flow. His spirits ran over. He was like a boy returning from his first college term. His very face wore the boy's open, innocent, earnest look that used to attract men to him in his first college year. His delight in the fields and woods, in the sweet country air and the sunlight, was without bound. How often had we driven this road together in the old days!

Every turn was familiar. The swamp where the tamaracks stood straight and slim out of their beds of moss; the brule, as we used to call it, where the pine-stumps, huge and blackened, were half-hidden by the new growth of poplars and soft maples; the big hill, where we used to get out and walk when the roads were bad; the orchards, where the harvest apples were best and most accessible--all had their memories.

It was one of those perfect afternoons that so often come in the early Canadian summer, before Nature grows weary with the heat. The white gravel road was trimmed on either side with turf of living green, close cropped by the sheep that wandered in flocks along its whole length. Beyond the picturesque snake-fences stretched the fields of springing grain, of varying shades of green, with here and there a dark brown patch, marking a turnip field or summer fallow, and far back were the woods of maple and beech and elm, with here and there the tufted top of a mighty pine, the lonely representative of a vanished race, standing clear above the humbler trees.

As we drove through the big swamp, where the yawning, haunted gully plunges down to its gloomy depths, Graeme reminded me of that night when our horse saw something in that same gully, and refused to go past; and I felt again, though it was broad daylight, something of the grue that shivered down my back, as I saw in the moonlight the gleam of a white thing far through the pine trunks.

As we came nearer home the houses became familiar. Every house had its tale: we had eaten or slept in most of them; we had sampled apples, and cherries, and plums from their orchards, openly as guests, or secretly as marauders, under cover of night--the more delightful way, I fear. Ah! happy days, with these innocent crimes and fleeting remorses, how bravely we faced them, and how gaily we lived them, and how yearningly we look back at them now! The sun was just dipping into the tree-tops of the distant woods behind as we came to the top of the last hill that overlooked the valley, in which lay the village of Riverdale. Wooded hills stood about it on three sides, and, where the hills faded out, there lay the mill-pond sleeping and smiling in the sun. Through the village ran the white road, up past the old frame church, and on to the white manse standing among the trees. That was Graeme's home, and mine too, for I had never known another worthy of the name. We held up our team to look down over the valley, with its rampart of wooded hills, its shining pond, and its nestling village, and on past to the church and the white manse, hiding among the trees. The beauty, the peace, the warm, loving homeliness of the scene came about our hearts, but, being men, we could find no words.

'Let's go,' cried Graeme, and down the hill we tore and rocked and swayed to the amazement of the steady team, whose education from the earliest years had impressed upon their minds the criminality of attempting to do anything but walk carefully down a hill, at least for two-thirds of the way. Through the village, in a cloud of dust, we swept, catching a glimpse of a well-known face here and there, and flinging a salutation as we passed, leaving the owner of the face rooted to his place in astonishment at the sight of Graeme whirling on in his old-time, well-known reckless manner. Only old Dunc. M'Leod was equal to the moment, for as Graeme called out, 'Hello, Dunc.!' the old man lifted up his hands, and called back in an awed voice: 'Bless my soul! is it yourself?'

'Stands his whisky well, poor old chap!' was Graeme's comment.

As we neared the church he pulled up his team, and we went quietly past the sleepers there, then again on the full run down the gentle slope, over the little brook, and up to the gate. He had hardly got his team pulled up before, flinging me the lines, he was out over the wheel, for coming down the walk, with her hands lifted high, was a dainty little lady, with the face of an angel. In a moment Graeme had her in his arms. I heard the faint cry, 'My boy, my boy,' and got down on the other side to attend to my off horse, surprised to find my hands trembling and my eyes full of tears. Back upon the steps stood an old gentleman, with white hair and flowing beard, handsome, straight, and stately--Graeme's father, waiting his turn.

'Welcome home, my lad,' was his greeting, as he kissed his son, and the tremor of his voice, and the sight of the two men kissing each other, like women, sent me again to my horses' heads.

'There's Connor, mother!' shouted out Graeme, and the dainty little lady, in her black silk and white lace, came out to me quickly, with outstretched hands.

'You, too, are welcome home,' she said, and kissed me.

I stood with my hat off, saying something about being glad to come, but wishing that I could get away before I should make quite a fool of myself. For as I looked down upon that beautiful face, pale, except for a faint flush upon each faded cheek, and read the story of pain endured and conquered, and as I thought of all the long years of waiting and of vain hoping, I found my throat dry and sore, and the words would not come. But her quick sense needed no words, and she came to my help.

'You will find Jack at the stable,' she said, smiling; 'he ought to have been here.'

The stable! Why had I not thought of that before? Thankfully now my words came--

'Yes, certainly, I'll find him, Mrs. Graeme. I suppose he's as much of a scapegrace as ever, and off I went to look up Graeme's young brother, who had given every promise in the old days of developing into as stirring a rascal as one could desire; but who, as I found out later, had not lived these years in his mother's home for nothing.

'Oh, Jack's a good boy,' she answered, smiling again, as she turned toward the other two, now waiting for her upon the walk.

The week that followed was a happy one for us all; but for the mother it was full to the brim with joy. Her sweet face was full of content, and in her eyes rested a great peace. Our days were spent driving about among the hills, or strolling through the maple woods, or down into the tamarack swamp, where the pitcher plants and the swamp lilies and the marigold waved above the deep moss. In the evenings we sat under the trees on the lawn till the stars came out and the night dews drove us in. Like two lovers, Graeme and his mother would wander off together, leaving Jack and me to each other. Jack was reading for divinity, and was really a fine, manly fellow, with all his brother's turn for rugby, and I took to him amazingly; but after the day was over we would gather about the supper table, and the talk would be of all things under heaven--art, football, theology. The mother would lead in all. How quick she was, how bright her fancy, how subtle her intellect, and through all a gentle grace, very winning and beautiful to see!

Do what I would, Graeme would talk little of the mountains and his life there.

'My lion will not roar, Mrs. Graeme,' I complained; 'he simply will not.'

'You should twist his tail,' said Jack.

'That seems to be the difficulty, Jack,' said his mother, 'to get hold of his tale.'

'Oh, mother,' groaned Jack; 'you never did such a thing before! How could you? Is it this baleful Western influence?'

'I shall reform, Jack,' she replied brightly.

'But, seriously, Graeme,' I remonstrated, 'you ought to tell your people of your life--that free, glorious life in the mountains.'

'Free! Glorious! To some men, perhaps!' said Graeme, and then fell into silence.

But I saw Graeme as a new man the night he talked theology with his father. The old minister was a splendid Calvinist, of heroic type, and as he discoursed of God's sovereignty and election, his face glowed and his voice rang out.

Graeme listened intently, now and then putting in a question, as one would a keen knife-thrust into a foe. But the old man knew his ground, and moved easily among his ideas, demolishing the enemy as he appeared, with jaunty grace. In the full flow of his triumphant argument, Graeme turned to him with sudden seriousness.

'Look here, father! I was born a Calvinist, and I can't see how any one with a level head can hold anything else, than that the Almighty has some idea as to how He wants to run His universe, and He means to carry out His idea, and is carrying it out; but what would you do in a case like this?' Then he told him the story of poor Billy Breen, his fight and his defeat.

'Would you preach election to that chap?'

The mother's eyes were shining with tears.

The old gentleman blew his nose like a trumpet, and then said gravely--

'No, my boy, you don't feed babes with meat. But what came to him?'

Then Graeme asked me to finish the tale. After I had finished the story of Billy's final triumph and of Craig's part in it, they sat long silent, till the minister, clearing his throat hard and blowing his nose more like a trumpet than ever, said with great emphasis--

'Thank God for such a man in such a place! I wish there were more of us like him.'

'I should like to see you out there, sir,' said Graeme admiringly; 'you'd get them, but you wouldn't have time for election.'

'Yes, yes!' said his father warmly; 'I should love to have a chance just to preach election to these poor lads. Would I were twenty years younger!'

'It is worth a man's life,' said Graeme earnestly. His younger brother turned his face eagerly toward the mother. For answer she slipped her hand into his and said softly, while her eyes shone like stars--

'Some day, Jack, perhaps! God knows.' But Jack only looked steadily at her, smiling a little and patting her hand.

'You'd shine there, mother,' said Graeme, smiling upon her; 'you'd better come with me.' She started, and said faintly--

'With you?' It was the first hint he had given of his purpose. 'You are going back?'

'What! as a missionary?' said Jack.

'Not to preach, Jack; I'm not orthodox enough,' looking at his father and shaking his head; 'but to build railroads and lend a hand to some poor chap, if I can.'

'Could you not find work nearer home, my boy?' asked the father; 'there is plenty of both kinds near us here, surely.'

'Lots of work, but not mine, I fear,' answered Graeme, keeping his eyes away from his mother's face. 'A man must do his own work.'

His voice was quiet and resolute, and glancing at the beautiful face at the end of the table, I saw in the pale lips and yearning eyes that the mother was offering up her firstborn, that ancient sacrifice. But not all the agony of sacrifice could wring from her entreaty or complaint in the hearing of her sons. That was for other ears and for the silent hours of the night. And next morning when she came down to meet us her face was wan and weary, but it wore the peace of victory and a glory not of earth. Her greeting was full of dignity, sweet and gentle; but when she came to Graeme she lingered over him and kissed him twice. And that was all that any of us ever saw of that sore fight.

At the end of the week I took leave of them, and last of all of the mother.

She hesitated just a moment, then suddenly put her hands upon my shoulders and kissed me, saying softly, 'You are his friend; you will sometimes come to me?'

'Gladly, if I may,' I hastened to answer, for the sweet, brave face was too much to bear; and, till she left us for that world of which she was a part, I kept my word, to my own great and lasting good. When Graeme met me in the city at the end of the summer, he brought me her love, and then burst forth--

'Connor, do you know, I have just discovered my mother! I have never known her till this summer.'

'More fool you,' I answered, for often had I, who had never known a mother, envied him his.

'Yes, that is true,' he answered slowly; 'but you cannot see until you have eyes.'

Before he set out again for the west I gave him a supper, asking the men who had been with us in the old 'Varsity days. I was doubtful as to the wisdom of this, and was persuaded only by Graeme's eager assent to my proposal.

'Certainly, let's have them,' he said; 'I shall be awfully glad to see them; great stuff they were.'

'But, I don't know, Graeme; you see--well--hang it!--you know--you're different, you know.'

He looked at me curiously.

'I hope I can still stand a good supper, and if the boys can't stand me, why, I can't help it. I'll do anything but roar, and don't you begin to work off your menagerie act--now, you hear me!'

'Well, it is rather hard lines that when I have been talking up my lion for a year, and then finally secure him, that he will not roar.'

'Serve you right,' he replied, quite heartlessly; 'but I'll tell you what I'll do, I'll feed! Don't you worry,' he adds soothingly; 'the supper will go.'

And go it did. The supper was of the best; the wines first-class. I had asked Graeme about the wines.

'Do as you like, old man,' was his answer; 'it's your supper, but,' he added, 'are the men all straight?'

I ran them over in my mind.

'Yes; I think so.'

If not, don't you help them down; and anyway, you can't be too careful. But don't mind me; I am quit of the whole business from this out.' So I ventured wines, for the last time, as it happened.

We were a quaint combination. Old 'Beetles,' whose nickname was prophetic of his future fame as a bugman, as the fellows irreverently said; 'Stumpy' Smith, a demon bowler; Polly Lindsay, slow as ever and as sure as when he held the half-back line with Graeme, and used to make my heart stand still with terror at his cool deliberation. But he was never known to fumble nor to funk, and somehow he always got us out safe enough. Then there was Rattray--'Rat' for short--who, from a swell, had developed into a cynic with a sneer, awfully clever and a good enough fellow at heart. Little 'Wig' Martin, the sharpest quarter ever seen, and big Barney Lundy, centre scrimmage, whose terrific roar and rush had often struck terror to the enemy's heart, and who was Graeme's slave. Such was the party.

As the supper went on my fears began to vanish, for if Graeme did not 'roar,' he did the next best thing--ate and talked quite up to his old form. Now we played our matches over again, bitterly lamenting the 'if's' that had lost us the championships, and wildly approving the tackles that had saved, and the runs that had made the 'Varsity crowd go mad with delight and had won for us. And as their names came up in talk, we learned how life had gone with those who had been our comrades of ten years ago. Some, success had lifted to high places; some, failure had left upon the rocks, and a few lay in their graves.

But as the evening wore on, I began to wish that I had left out the wines, for the men began to drop an occasional oath, though I had let them know during the summer that Graeme was not the man he had been. But Graeme smoked and talked and heeded not, till Rattray swore by that name most sacred of all ever borne by man. Then Graeme opened upon him in a cool, slow way--

'What an awful fool a man is, to damn things as you do, Rat. Things are not damned. It is men who are; and that is too bad to be talked much about but when a man flings out of his foul mouth the name of Jesus Christ'--here he lowered his voice--'it's a shame--it's more, it's a crime.'

There was dead silence, then Rattray replied--

'I suppose you're right enough, it is bad form; but crime is rather strong, I think.'

'Not if you consider who it is,' said Graeme with emphasis.

'Oh, come now,' broke in Beetles. 'Religion is all right, is a good thing, and I believe a necessary thing for the race, but no one takes seriously any longer the Christ myth.'

'What about your mother, Beetles?' put in Wig Martin.

Beetles consigned him to the pit and was silent, for his father was an Episcopal clergyman, and his mother a saintly woman.

'I fooled with that for some time, Beetles, but it won't do. You can't build a religion that will take the devil out of a man on a myth. That won't do the trick. I don't want to argue about it, but I am quite convinced the myth theory is not reasonable, and besides, it wont work.'

'Will the other work?' asked Rattray, with a sneer.

'Sure!' said Grame; 'I've seen it.'

'Where?' challenged Rattray. 'I haven't seen much of it.'

'Yes, you have, Rattray, you know you have,' said Wig again. But Rattray ignored him.

'I'll tell you, boys,' said Graeme. 'I want you to know, anyway, why I believe what I do.'

Then he told them the story of old man Nelson, from the old coast days, before I knew him, to the end. He told the story well. The stern fight and the victory of the life, and the self-sacrifice and the pathos of the death appealed to these men, who loved fight and could understand sacrifice.

'That's why I believe in Jesus Christ, and that's why I think it a crime to fling His name about!'

'I wish to Heaven I could say that,' said Beetles.

'Keep wishing hard enough and it will come to you,' said Graeme.

'Look here, old chap,' said Rattray; 'you're quite right about this; I'm willing to own up. Wig is correct. I know a few, at least, of that stamp, but most of those who go in for that sort of thing are not much account'

'For ten years, Rattray,' said Graeme in a downright, matter-of-fact way, 'you and I have tried this sort of thing'--tapping a bottle--'and we got out of it all there is to be got, paid well for it, too, and--faugh! you know it's not good enough, and the more you go in for it, the more you curse yourself. So I have quit this and I am going in for the other.'

'What! going in for preaching?'

'Not much--railroading--money in it--and lending a hand to fellows on the rocks.'

'I say, don't you want a centre forward?' said big Barney in his deep voice.

'Every man must play his game in his place, old chap. I'd like to see you tackle it, though, right well,' said Graeme earnestly. And so he did, in the after years, and good tackling it was. But that is another story.

'But, I say, Graeme,' persisted Beetles, 'about this business, do you mean to say you go the whole thing--Jonah, you know, and the rest of it?'

Graeme hesitated, then said--

'I haven't much of a creed, Beetles; don't really know how much I believe. But,' by this time he was standing, 'I do know that good is good, and bad is bad, and good and bad are not the same. And I know a man's a fool to follow the one, and a wise man to follow the other, and,' lowering his voice, 'I believe God is at the back of a man who wants to get done with bad. I've tried all that folly,' sweeping his hand over the glasses and bottles, 'and all that goes with it, and I've done with it'

'I'll go you that far,' roared big Barney, following his old captain as of yore.

'Good man,' said Graeme, striking hands with him.

'Put me down,' said little Wig cheerfully.

Then I took up the word, for there rose before me the scene in the League saloon, and I saw the beautiful face with the deep shining eyes, and I was speaking for her again. I told them of Craig and his fight for these men's lives. I told them, too, of how I had been too indolent to begin. 'But,' I said, 'I am going this far from to-night,' and I swept the bottles into the champagne tub.

'I say,' said Polly Lindsay, coming up in his old style, slow but sure, 'let's all go in, say for five years.' And so we did. We didn't sign anything, but every man shook hands with Graeme.

And as I told Craig about this a year later, when he was on his way back from his Old Land trip to join Graeme in the mountains, he threw up his head in the old way and said, 'It was well done. It must have been worth seeing. Old man Nelson's work is not done yet. Tell me again,' and he made me go over the whole scene with all the details put in.

But when I told Mrs. Mavor, after two years had gone, she only said, 'Old things are passed away, all things are become new'; but the light glowed in her eyes till I could not see their colour. But all that, too, is another story.

CHAPTER XV
COMING TO THEIR OWN

A man with a conscience is often provoking, sometimes impossible. Persuasion is lost upon him. He will not get angry, and he looks at one with such a far-away expression in his face that in striving to persuade him one feels earthly and even fiendish. At least this was my experience with Craig. He spent a week with me just before he sailed for the Old Land, for the purpose, as he said, of getting some of the coal dust and other grime out of him.

He made me angry the last night of his stay, and all the more that he remained quite sweetly unmoved. It was a strategic mistake of mine to tell him how Nelson came home to us, and how Graeme stood up before the 'Varsity chaps at my supper and made his confession and confused Rattray's easy-stepping profanity, and started his own five-year league. For all this stirred in Craig the hero, and he was ready for all sorts of heroic nonsense, as I called it. We talked of everything but the one thing, and about that we said not a word till, bending low to poke my fire and to hide my face, I plunged--

'You will see her, of course?'

He made no pretence of not understanding but answered--

'Of course.'

'There's really no sense in her staying over there,' I suggested.

'And yet she is a wise woman,' he said, as if carefully considering the question.

'Heaps of landlords never see their tenants, and they are none the worse.'

'The landlords?'

'No, the tenants.'

'Probably, having such landlords.'

'And as for the old lady, there must be some one in the connection to whom it would be a Godsend to care for her.'

'Now, Connor,' he said quietly, 'don't. We have gone over all there is to be said. Nothing new has come. Don't turn it all up again.'

Then I played the heathen and raged, as Graeme would have said, till Craig smiled a little wearily and said--

'You exhaust yourself, old chap. Have a pipe, do'; and after a pause he added in his own way, 'What would you have? The path lies straight from my feet. Should I quit it? I could not so disappoint you--and all of them.'

And I knew he was thinking of Graeme and the lads in the mountains he had taught to be true men. It did not help my rage, but it checked my speech; so I smoked in silence till he was moved to say--

'And after all, you know, old chap, there are great compensations for all losses; but for the loss of a good conscience towards God, what can make up?'

But, all the same, I hoped for some better result from his visit to Britain. It seemed to me that something must turn up to change such an unbearable situation.

The year passed, however, and when I looked into Craig's face again I knew that nothing had been changed, and that he had come back to take up again his life alone, more resolutely hopeful than ever.

But the year had left its mark upon him too. He was a broader and deeper man. He had been living and thinking with men of larger ideas and richer culture, and he was far too quick in sympathy with life to remain untouched by his surroundings. He was more tolerant of opinions other than his own, but more unrelenting in his fidelity to conscience and more impatient of half-heartedness and self-indulgence. He was full of reverence for the great scholars and the great leaders of men he had come to know.

'Great, noble fellows they are, and extraordinarily modest,' he said--'that is, the really great are modest. There are plenty of the other sort, neither great nor modest. And the books to be read! I am quite hopeless about my reading. It gave me a queer sensation to shake hands with a man who had written a great book. To hear him make commonplace remarks, to witness a faltering in knowledge--one expects these men to know everything--and to experience respectful kindness at his hands!'

'What of the younger men?' I asked.

'Bright, keen, generous fellows. In things theoretical, omniscient; but in things practical, quite helpless. They toss about great ideas as the miners lumps of coal. They can call them by their book names easily enough, but I often wondered whether they could put them into English. Some of them I coveted for the mountains. Men with clear heads and big hearts, and built after Sandy M'Naughton's model. It does seem a sinful waste of God's good human stuff to see these fellows potter away their lives among theories living and dead, and end up by producing a book! They are all either making or going to make a book. A good thing we haven't to read them. But here and there among them is some quiet chap who will make a book that men will tumble over each other to read.'

Then we paused and looked at each other.

'Well?' I said. He understood me.

'Yes!' he answered slowly, 'doing great work. Every one worships her just as we do, and she is making them all do something worth while, as she used to make us.'

He spoke cheerfully and readily as if he were repeating a lesson well learned, but he could not humbug me. I felt the heartache in the cheerful tone.

'Tell me about her,' I said, for I knew that if he would talk it would do him good. And talk he did, often forgetting me, till, as I listened, I found myself looking again into the fathomless eyes, and hearing again the heart-searching voice. I saw her go in and out of the little red-tiled cottages and down the narrow back lanes of the village; I heard her voice in a sweet, low song by the bed of a dying child, or pouring forth floods of music in the great new hall of the factory town near by. But I could not see, though he tried to show me, the stately gracious lady receiving the country folk in her home. He did not linger over that scene, but went back again to the gate-cottage where she had taken him one day to see Billy Breen's mother.

'I found the old woman knew all about me,' he said, simply enough; 'but there were many things about Billy she had never heard, and I was glad to put her right on some points, though Mrs. Mavor would not hear it.'

He sat silent for a little, looking into the coals; then went on in a soft, quiet voice--

'It brought back the mountains and the old days to hear again Billy's tones in his mother's voice, and to see her sitting there in the very dress she wore the night of the League, you remember--some soft stuff with black lace about it--and to hear her sing as she did for Billy--ah! ah!' His voice unexpectedly broke, but in a moment he was master of himself and begged me to forgive his weakness. I am afraid I said words that should not be said--a thing I never do, except when suddenly and utterly upset.

'I am getting selfish and weak,' he said; 'I must get to work. I am glad to get to work. There is much to do, and it is worth while, if only to keep one from getting useless and lazy.'

'Useless and lazy!' I said to myself, thinking of my life beside his, and trying to get command of my voice, so as not to make quite a fool of myself. And for many a day those words goaded me to work and to the exercise of some mild self-denial. But more than all else, after Craig had gone back to the mountains, Graeme's letters from the railway construction camp stirred one to do unpleasant duty long postponed, and rendered uncomfortable my hours of most luxurious ease. Many of the old gang were with him, both of lumbermen and miners, and Craig was their minister. And the letters told of how he laboured by day and by night along the line of construction, carrying his tent and kit with him, preaching straight sermons, watching by sick men, writing their letters, and winning their hearts; making strong their lives, and helping them to die well when their hour came. One day, these letters proved too much for me, and I packed away my paints and brushes, and made my vow unto the Lord that I would be 'useless and lazy' no longer, but would do something with myself. In consequence, I found myself within three weeks walking the London hospitals, finishing my course, that I might join that band of men who were doing something with life, or, if throwing it away, were not losing it for nothing. I had finished being a fool, I hoped, at least a fool of the useless and luxurious kind. The letter that came from Graeme, in reply to my request for a position on his staff, was characteristic of the man, both new and old, full of gayest humour and of most earnest welcome to the work.

Mrs. Mavor's reply was like herself--

'I knew you would not long be content with the making of pictures, which the world does not really need, and would join your friends in the dear West, making lives that the world needs so sorely.'

But her last words touched me strangely--

'But be sure to be thankful every day for your privilege. . . . It will be good to think of you all, with the glorious mountains about you, and Christ's own work in your hands. . . . Ah! how we would like to choose our work, and the place in which to do it!'

The longing did not appear in the words, but I needed no words to tell me how deep and how constant it was. And I take some credit to myself, that in my reply I gave her no bidding to join our band, but rather praised the work she was doing in her place, telling her how I had heard of it from Craig.

The summer found me religiously doing Paris and Vienna, gaining a more perfect acquaintance with the extent and variety of my own ignorance, and so fully occupied in this interesting and wholesome occupation that I fell out with all my correspondents, with the result of weeks of silence between us.

Two letters among the heap waiting on my table in London made my heart beat quick, but with how different feelings: one from Graeme telling me that Craig had been very ill, and that he was to take him home as soon as he could be moved. Mrs. Mavor's letter told me of the death of the old lady, who had been her care for the past two years, and of her intention to spend some months in her old home in Edinburgh. And this letter it is that accounts for my presence in a miserable, dingy, dirty little hall running off a close in the historic Cowgate, redolent of the glories of the splendid past, and of the various odours of the evil-smelling present. I was there to hear Mrs. Mavor sing to the crowd of gamins that thronged the closes in the neighbourhood, and that had been gathered into a club by 'a fine leddie frae the West End,' for the love of Christ and His lost. This was an 'At Home' night, and the mothers and fathers, sisters and brothers, of all ages and sizes were present. Of all the sad faces I had ever seen, those mothers carried the saddest and most woe-stricken. 'Heaven pity us!' I found myself saying; 'is this the beautiful, the cultured, the heaven-exalted city of Edinburgh? Will it not, for this, be cast down into hell some day, if it repent not of its closes and their dens of defilement? Oh! the utter weariness, the dazed hopelessness of the ghastly faces! Do not the kindly, gentle church-going folk of the crescents and the gardens see them in their dreams, or are their dreams too heavenly for these ghastly faces to appear?'

I cannot recall the programme of the evening, but in my memory-gallery is a vivid picture of that face, sweet, sad, beautiful, alight with the deep glow of her eyes, as she stood and sang to that dingy crowd. As I sat upon the window-ledge listening to the voice with its flowing song, my thoughts were far away, and I was looking down once more upon the eager, coal-grimed faces in the rude little church in Black Rock. I was brought back to find myself swallowing hard by an audible whisper from a wee lassie to her mother--

'Mither! See till yon man. He's greetin'.'

When I came to myself she was singing 'The Land o' the Leal,' the Scotch 'Jerusalem the Golden,' immortal, perfect. It needed experience of the hunger-haunted Cowgate closes, chill with the black mist of an eastern haar, to feel the full bliss of the vision in the words--

    'There's nae sorrow there, Jean,   There's neither cauld nor care, Jean,
The day is aye fair in The Land o' the Leal.'

A land of fair, warm days, untouched by sorrow and care, would be heaven indeed to the dwellers of the Cowgate.

The rest of that evening is hazy enough to me now, till I find myself opposite Mrs. Mavor at her fire, reading Graeme's letter; then all is vivid again.

I could not keep the truth from her. I knew it would be folly to try. So I read straight on till I came to the words--

'He has had mountain fever, whatever that may be, and he will not pull up again. If I can, I shall take him home to my mother'--when she suddenly stretched out her hand, saying, 'Oh, let me read!' and I gave her the letter. In a minute she had read it, and began almost breathlessly--

'Listen! my life is much changed. My mother-in-law is gone; she needs me no longer. My solicitor tells me, too, that owing to unfortunate investments there is need of money, so great need, that it is possible that either the estates or the works must go. My cousin has his all in the works--iron works, you know. It would be wrong to have him suffer. I shall give up the estates--that is best.' She paused.

'And come with me,' I cried.

'When do you sail?'

'Next week,' I answered eagerly.

She looked at me a few moments, and into her eyes there came a light soft and tender, as she said--

'I shall go with you.'

And so she did; and no old Roman in all the glory of a Triumph carried a prouder heart than I, as I bore her and her little one from the train to Graeme's carriage, crying--

'I've got her.'

But his was the better sense, for he stood waving his hat and shouting--

'He's all right,' at which Mrs. Mavor grew white; but when she shook hands with him, the red was in her cheek again.

'It was the cable did it,' went on Graeme. 'Connor's a great doctor! His first case will make him famous. Good prescription--after mountain fever try a cablegram!'

And the red grew deeper in the beautiful face beside us.

Never did the country look so lovely. The woods were in their gayest autumn dress; the brown fields were bathed in a purple haze; the air was sweet and fresh with a suspicion of the coming frosts of winter. But in spite of all the road seemed long, and it was as if hours had gone before our eyes fell upon the white manse standing among the golden leaves.

'Let them go,' I cried, as Graeme paused to take in the view, and down the sloping dusty road we flew on the dead run.

'Reminds one a little of Abe's curves,' said Graeme, as we drew up at the gate. But I answered him not, for I was introducing to each other the two best women in the world. As I was about to rush into the house, Graeme seized me by the collar, saying--

'Hold on, Connor! you forget your place, you're next.'

'Why, certainly,' I cried, thankfully enough; 'what an ass I am!'

'Quite true,' said Graeme solemnly.

'Where is he?' I asked.

'At this present moment?' he asked, in a shocked voice. 'Why, Connor, you surprise me.'

'Oh, I see!'

'Yes,' he went on gravely; 'you may trust my mother to be discreetly attending to her domestic duties; she is a great woman, my mother.'

I had no doubt of it, for at that moment she came out to us with little Marjorie in her arms.

'You have shown Mrs. Mavor to her room, mother, I hope,' said Graeme; but she only smiled and said--

'Run away with your horses, you silly boy,' at which he solemnly shook his head. 'Ah, mother, you are deep--who would have thought it of you?'

That evening the manse overflowed with joy, and the days that followed were like dreams set to sweet music.

But for sheer wild delight, nothing in my memory can quite come up to the demonstration organised by Graeme, with assistance from Nixon, Shaw, Sandy, Abe, Geordie, and Baptiste, in honour of the arrival in camp of Mr. and Mrs. Craig. And, in my opinion, it added something to the occasion, that after all the cheers for

Mr. and Mrs. Craig had died away, and after all the hats had come down, Baptiste, who had never taken his eyes from that radiant face, should suddenly have swept the crowd into a perfect storm of cheers by excitedly seizing his tuque, and calling out in his shrill voice--

'By gar! Tree cheer for Mrs. Mavor.'

And for many a day the men of Black Rock would easily fall into the old and well-loved name; but up and down the line of construction, in all the camps beyond the Great Divide, the new name became as dear as the old had ever been in Black Rock.

Those old wild days are long since gone into the dim distance of the past. They will not come again, for we have fallen into quiet times; but often in my quietest hours I feel my heart pause in its beat to hear again that strong, clear voice, like the sound of a trumpet, bidding us to be men; and I think of them all--Graeme, their chief, Sandy, Baptiste, Geordie, Abe, the Campbells, Nixon, Shaw, all stronger, better for their knowing of him, and then I think of Billy asleep under the pines, and of old man Nelson with the long grass waving over him in the quiet churchyard, and all my nonsense leaves me, and I bless the Lord for all His benefits, but chiefly for the day I met the missionary of Black Rock in the lumber-camp among the Selkirks.

The Codes Of Hammurabi And Moses
W. W. Davies

QTY

The discovery of the Hammurabi Code is one of the greatest achievements of archaeology, and is of paramount interest, not only to the student of the Bible, but also to all those interested in ancient history...

Religion   **ISBN:** *1-59462-338-4*   **Pages:132**

MSRP $12.95

The Theory of Moral Sentiments
Adam Smith

QTY

This work from 1749. contains original theories of conscience amd moral judgment and it is the foundation for systemof morals.

Philosophy **ISBN:** *1-59462-777-0*   **Pages:536**

MSRP $19.95

Jessica's First Prayer
Hesba Stretton

QTY

In a screened and secluded corner of one of the many railway-bridges which span the streets of London there could be seen a few years ago, from five o'clock every morning until half past eight, a tidily set-out coffee-stall, consisting of a trestle and board, upon which stood two large tin cans, with a small fire of charcoal burning under each so as to keep the coffee boiling during the early hours of the morning when the work-people were thronging into the city on their way to their daily toil...

Childrens   **ISBN:** *1-59462-373-2*

Pages:84

MSRP $9.95

My Life and Work
Henry Ford

QTY

Henry Ford revolutionized the world with his implementation of mass production for the Model T automobile. Gain valuable business insight into his life and work with his own auto-biography... "We have only started on our development of our country we have not as yet, with all our talk of wonderful progress, done more than scratch the surface. The progress has been wonderful enough but..."

Biographies/   **ISBN:** *1-59462-198-5*

Pages:300

MSRP $21.95

The Art of Cross-Examination
Francis Wellman

QTY

I presume it is the experience of every author, after his first book is published upon an important subject, to be almost overwhelmed with a wealth of ideas and illustrations which could readily have been included in his book, and which to his own mind, at least, seem to make a second edition inevitable. Such certainly was the case with me; and when the first edition had reached its sixth impression in five months, I rejoiced to learn that it seemed to my publishers that the book had met with a sufficiently favorable reception to justify a second and considerably enlarged edition. ..

Reference   ISBN: *1-59462-647-2*

Pages:412

MSRP $19.95

On the Duty of Civil Disobedience
Henry David Thoreau

QTY

Thoreau wrote his famous essay, On the Duty of Civil Disobedience, as a protest against an unjust but popular war and the immoral but popular institution of slave-owning. He did more than write—he declined to pay his taxes, and was hauled off to gaol in consequence. Who can say how much this refusal of his hastened the end of the war and of slavery ?

Law   ISBN: *1-59462-747-9*   **Pages:48**

MSRP $7.45

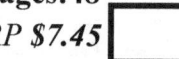

Dream Psychology Psychoanalysis for Beginners
Sigmund Freud

QTY

Sigmund Freud, born Sigismund Schlomo Freud (May 6, 1856 - September 23, 1939), was a Jewish-Austrian neurologist and psychiatrist who co-founded the psychoanalytic school of psychology. Freud is best known for his theories of the unconscious mind, especially involving the mechanism of repression; his redefinition of sexual desire as mobile and directed towards a wide variety of objects; and his therapeutic techniques, especially his understanding of transference in the therapeutic relationship and the presumed value of dreams as sources of insight into unconscious desires.

Pages:196

Psychology   ISBN: *1-59462-905-6*

MSRP $15.45

The Miracle of Right Thought
Orison Swett Marden

QTY

Believe with all of your heart that you will do what you were made to do. When the mind has once formed the habit of holding cheerful, happy, prosperous pictures, it will not be easy to form the opposite habit. It does not matter how improbable or how far away this realization may see, or how dark the prospects may be, if we visualize them as best we can, as vividly as possible, hold tenaciously to them and vigorously struggle to attain them, they will gradually become actualized, realized in the life. But a desire, a longing without endeavor, a yearning abandoned or held indifferently will vanish without realization.

Pages:360

Self Help   ISBN: *1-59462-644-8*

MSRP $25.45

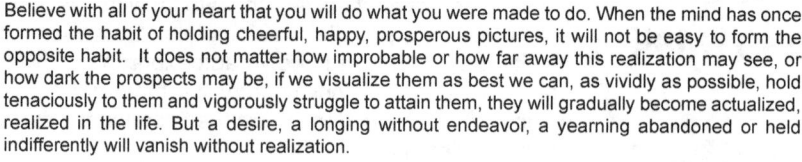

QTY

The Rosicrucian Cosmo-Conception Mystic Christianity *by Max Heindel* ISBN: *1-59462-188-8* **$38.95**
The Rosicrucian Cosmo-conception is not dogmatic, neither does it appeal to any other authority than the reason of the student. It is: not controversial, but is: sent forth in the, hope that it may help to clear... New Age/Religion Pages 646

Abandonment To Divine Providence *by Jean-Pierre de Caussade* ISBN: *1-59462-228-0* **$25.95**
"The Rev. Jean Pierre de Caussade was one of the most remarkable spiritual writers of the Society of Jesus in France in the 18th Century. His death took place at Toulouse in 1751. His works have gone through many editions and have been republished... Inspirational/Religion Pages 400

Mental Chemistry *by Charles Haanel* ISBN: *1-59462-192-6* **$23.95**
Mental Chemistry allows the change of material conditions by combining and appropriately utilizing the power of the mind. Much like applied chemistry creates something new and unique out of careful combinations of chemicals the mastery of mental chemistry... New Age/Business Pages 354

The Letters of Robert Browning and Elizabeth Barret Barrett 1845-1846 vol II ISBN: *1-59462-193-4* **$35.95**
by Robert Browning and Elizabeth Barrett Biographies Pages 596

Gleanings In Genesis (volume I) *by Arthur W. Pink* ISBN: *1-59462-130-6* **$27.45**
Appropriately has Genesis been termed "the seed plot of the Bible" for in it we have, in germ form, almost all of the great doctrines which are afterwards fully developed in the books of Scripture which follow... Religion/Inspirational Pages 420

The Master Key *by L. W. de Laurence* ISBN: *1-59462-001-6* **$30.95**
In no branch of human knowledge has there been a more lively increase of the spirit of research during the past few years than in the study of Psychology, Concentration and Mental Discipline. The requests for authentic lessons in Thought Control, Mental Discipline and... New Age/Business Pages 422

The Lesser Key Of Solomon Goetia *by L. W. de Laurence* ISBN: *1-59462-092-X* **$9.95**
This translation of the first book of the "Lernegton" which is now for the first time made accessible to students of Talismanic Magic was done, after careful collation and edition, from numerous Ancient Manuscripts in Hebrew, Latin, and French... New Age/Occult Pages 92

Rubaiyat Of Omar Khayyam *by Edward Fitzgerald* ISBN:*1-59462-332-5* **$13.95**
Edward Fitzgerald, whom the world has already learned, in spite of his own efforts to remain within the shadow of anonymity, to look upon as one of the rarest poets of the century, was born at Bredfield, in Suffolk, on the 31st of March, 1809. He was the third son of John Purcell... Music Pages 172

Ancient Law *by Henry Maine* ISBN: *1-59462-128-4* **$29.95**
The chief object of the following pages is to indicate some of the earliest ideas of mankind, as they are reflected in Ancient Law, and to point out the relation of those ideas to modern thought. Religion/History Pages 452

Far-Away Stories *by William J. Locke* ISBN: *1-59462-129-2* **$19.45**
"Good wine needs no bush, but a collection of mixed vintages does. And this book is just such a collection. Some of the stories I do not want to remain buried for ever in the museum files of dead magazine-numbers an author's not unpardonable vanity..." Fiction Pages 272

Life of David Crockett *by David Crockett* ISBN: *1-59462-250-7* **$27.45**
"Colonel David Crockett was one of the most remarkable men of the times in which he lived. Born in humble life, but gifted with a strong will, an indomitable courage, and unremitting perseverance... Biographies/New Age Pages 424

Lip-Reading *by Edward Nitchie* ISBN: *1-59462-206-X* **$25.95**
Edward B. Nitchie, founder of the New York School for the Hard of Hearing, now the Nitchie School of Lip-Reading, Inc, wrote "LIP-READING Principles and Practice". The development and perfecting of this meritorious work on lip-reading was an undertaking... How-to Pages 400

A Handbook of Suggestive Therapeutics, Applied Hypnotism, Psychic Science ISBN: *1-59462-214-0* **$24.95**
by Henry Munro Health/New Age/Health/Self-help Pages 376

A Doll's House: and Two Other Plays *by Henrik Ibsen* ISBN: *1-59462-112-8* **$19.95**
Henrik Ibsen created this classic when in revolutionary 1848 Rome. Introducing some striking concepts in playwriting for the realist genre, this play has been studied the world over. Fiction/Classics/Plays 308

The Light of Asia *by sir Edwin Arnold* ISBN: *1-59462-204-3* **$13.95**
In this poetic masterpiece, Edwin Arnold describes the life and teachings of Buddha. The man who was to become known as Buddha to the world was born as Prince Gautama of India but he rejected the worldly riches and abandoned the reigns of power when... Religion/History/Biographies Pages 170

The Complete Works of Guy de Maupassant *by Guy de Maupassant* ISBN: *1-59462-157-8* **$16.95**
"For days and days, nights and nights, I had dreamed of that first kiss which was to consecrate our engagement, and I knew not on what spot I should put my lips..." Fiction/Classics Pages 240

The Art of Cross-Examination *by Francis L. Wellman* ISBN: *1-59462-309-0* **$26.95**
Written by a renowned trial lawyer, Wellman imparts his experience and uses case studies to explain how to use psychology to extract desired information through questioning. How-to/Science/Reference Pages 408

Answered or Unanswered? *by Louisa Vaughan* ISBN: *1-59462-248-5* **$10.95**
Miracles of Faith in China Religion Pages 112

The Edinburgh Lectures on Mental Science (1909) *by Thomas* ISBN: *1-59462-008-3* **$11.95**
This book contains the substance of a course of lectures recently given by the writer in the Queen Street Hall, Edinburgh. Its purpose is to indicate the Natural Principles governing the relation between Mental Action and Material Conditions... New Age/Psychology Pages 148

Ayesha *by H. Rider Haggard* ISBN: *1-59462-301-5* **$24.95**
Verily and indeed it is the unexpected that happens! Probably if there was one person upon the earth from whom the Editor of this, and of a certain previous history, did not expect to hear again... Classics Pages 380

Ayala's Angel *by Anthony Trollope* ISBN: *1-59462-352-X* **$29.95**
The two girls were both pretty, but Lucy who was twenty-one who supposed to be simple and comparatively unattractive, whereas Ayala was credited, as her Bombwhat romantic name might show, with poetic charm and a taste for romance. Ayala when her father died was nineteen... Fiction Pages 484

The American Commonwealth *by James Bryce* ISBN: *1-59462-286-8* **$34.45**
An interpretation of American democratic political theory. It examines political mechanics and society from the perspective of Scotsman James Bryce Politics Pages 572

Stories of the Pilgrims *by Margaret P. Pumphrey* ISBN: *1-59462-116-0* **$17.95**
This book explores pilgrims religious oppression in England as well as their escape to Holland and eventual crossing to America on the Mayflower, and their early days in New England... History Pages 268

www.bookjungle.com *email: sales@bookjungle.com fax: 630-214-0564 mail: Book Jungle PO Box 2226 Champaign, IL 61825*

QTY

The Fasting Cure *by Sinclair Upton*   **ISBN:** *1-59462-222-1*   **$13.95**

In the Cosmopolitan Magazine for May, 1910, and in the Contemporary Review (London) for April, 1910, I published an article dealing with my experiences in fasting. I have written a great many magazine articles, but never one which attracted so much attention... New Age/Self Help/Health Pages 164

Hebrew Astrology *by Sepharial*   **ISBN:** *1-59462-308-2*   **$13.45**

In these days of advanced thinking it is a matter of common observation that we have left many of the old landmarks behind and that we are now pressing forward to greater heights and to a wider horizon than that which represented the mind-content of our progenitors... Astrology Pages 144

Thought Vibration or The Law of Attraction in the Thought World   **ISBN:** *1-59462-127-6*   **$12.95**

by William Walker Atkinson   Psychology/Religion Pages 144

Optimism *by Helen Keller*   **ISBN:** *1-59462-108-X*   **$15.95**

Helen Keller was blind, deaf, and mute since 19 months old, yet famously learned how to overcome these handicaps, communicate with the world, and spread her lectures promoting optimism. An inspiring read for everyone... Biographies/Inspirational Pages 84

Sara Crewe *by Frances Burnett*   **ISBN:** *1-59462-360-0*   **$9.45**

In the first place, Miss Minchin lived in London. Her home was a large, dull, tall one, in a large, dull square, where all the houses were alike, and all the sparrows were alike, and where all the door-knockers made the same heavy sound... Childrens/Classic Pages 88

The Autobiography of Benjamin Franklin *by Benjamin Franklin*   **ISBN:** *1-59462-135-7*   **$24.95**

The Autobiography of Benjamin Franklin has probably been more extensively read than any other American historical work, and no other book of its kind has had such ups and downs of fortune. Franklin lived for many years in England, where he was agent... Biographies/History Pages 332

Name	
Email	
Telephone	
Address	
City, State ZIP	

☐ **Credit Card**   ☐ **Check / Money Order**

Credit Card Number	
Expiration Date	
Signature	

Please Mail to: Book Jungle
                 PO Box 2226
                 Champaign, IL 61825
or Fax to: 630-214-0564

ORDERING INFORMATION

web: *www.bookjungle.com*
email: *sales@bookjungle.com*
fax: *630-214-0564*
mail: *Book Jungle PO Box 2226 Champaign, IL 61825*
or PayPal *to sales@bookjungle.com*

Please contact us for bulk discounts

DIRECT-ORDER TERMS

**20% Discount if You Order
Two or More Books**
Free Domestic Shipping!
Accepted: Master Card, Visa,
Discover, American Express